MOTHERS

Chris Power lives and works in London. His column, 'A Brief Survey of the Short Story' has appeared in the *Guardian* since 2007. He has written for the BBC, the *New York Times* and the *New Statesman*. His fiction has been published in *Granta*, *The Stinging Fly*, *The Dublin Review* and *The White Review*, and broadcast on BBC Radio 4. *Mothers* is his first book.

Further praise for *Mothers*:

'Ten richly imagined, superbly controlled stories . . . ['Summer 76'] is marked by a simplicity and clarity of detail reminiscent of Alice Munro . . . ['Run'] recalls the lucid asperity of James Salter.' *Times Literary Supplement*

'The quietness of Power's approach, or rather the studiousness of it, can be exemplary. 'The Colossus of Rhodes', exploring the unreliability of memory and how storytelling can be a means of anaesthetising trauma, is strong enough to be taught as a masterclass in the form.' *Spectator*

'Power has an intelligent and confidently idiosyncratic approach to the form . . . His images are sharply drawn and often haunting. There is an obsessive quality to the

best of these stories that makes them feel pregnant with inscrutable meaning. Many of them have the bittersweet mood, the uncanny logic and the peculiar sheen of childhood memory . . . It is testament to the depth and distinctiveness of Power's characters that it seems so important to try to understand them, even as they fail to understand themselves.' *Sunday Times*

'In these stories of quiet desperation, there is the constant threat that psychosis is just around the corner, and we are left with the unsettling question of whether the past will inevitably catch up with us.' *Observer*

'Unsettling . . . These are strange stories, forbidding and unnerving, which need to be read carefully with an ear trained to what isn't being said, what isn't being heard.' *Financial Times*

'In Power's remarkable debut, he depicts mood, happenstance, self-deception and epiphany as well as any of his heroes. In using studied artifice, leaving out everything extraneous, he reveals life's complexity: the very chaos that we reckon with by telling stories.' *New Statesman*

'Gravely beautiful stories.' *Daily Mail*

'The most flipping wonderful debut collection I've read,

umm, ever? Hugely humane, super satisfying, gigantically accomplished.' Tanya Andrews, Director, Small Wonder Short Story Festival

'A uniquely unsettling and subtle debut collection.' *Guardian*

'The best, most accurate, most moving presentation of depression I have ever read in literature.' John Mitchinson, *Backlisted Podcast*

'Shocking and tender.' *Evening Standard*

'A collection of beautifully controlled stories that depict how the most powerful moments in our lives can be the most inexplicable or enigmatic. Power's characters are rootless, vigilant, and warily tuned to the limitations of their own self-knowledge.' Colin Barrett, author of *Young Skins*, winner of the *Guardian* First Book Award

'I am enormously admiring of the way the collection works together as a whole. But more than admiring: I was so moved by Power's vision, the intelligence, the sensitivity and close observation . . . All of these are so terrific! 'The Haväng Dolmen' so spooky and compelling; 'Run' a brilliant through-line of suspense with such a great ending; 'Johnny Kingdom', gosh, what a totally startling, funny, weird story. But honestly, I loved them all. I think Chris Power deserves every single laurel that comes his way.' Erica Wagner

'*Mothers* takes a theme too complex to approach except obliquely – the conflict between love and freedom – and, like a particle accelerator, repeatedly fires ideas at it to see what can be inferred from the collision. Power writes mothers, but also daughters, sons, lovers, families and bickering couples, testing different ages, sexualities, genders and cultures to create a composite which arrives at more than the sum of its parts – not a clutch of episodes, but a single, unified, many-sided work, best read cover to cover.' *White Review*

'These stories are really tightly coiled and finely crafted . . . The prose has this lacerating sadness to it, it really gets under the skin.' *Monocle Arts Review*

MOTHERS

Chris Power

FABER & FABER

First published in 2018
by Faber & Faber Limited
Bloomsbury House
74–77 Great Russell Street
London, WC1B 3DA
This paperback edition first published in 2019

Typeset by Faber & Faber Limited
Printed in the UK by CPI Group (UK) Ltd, Croydon, CR0 4YY

All rights reserved
© Chris Power, 2018

The right of Chris Power to be identified as author of this work
has been asserted in accordance with Section 77 of the Copyright,
Designs and Patents Act 1988

Earlier versions of 'Innsbruck' and 'Run' appeared in
The Dublin Review and *The Stinging Fly*.
'Johnny Kingdom' has appeared in *Granta*.

*Every effort has been made to trace or contact the copyright holders.
The publishers would be pleased to rectify at the earliest opportunity
any omissions or errors brought to their notice.*

*This book is sold subject to the condition that it shall not, by way of trade
or otherwise, be lent, resold, hired out or otherwise circulated without the
publisher's prior consent in any form of binding or cover other than that
in which it is published and without a similar condition including this
condition being imposed on the subsequent purchaser*

A CIP record for this book
is available from the British Library

ISBN 978-0-571-33969-3

2 4 6 8 10 9 7 5 3 1

For Mary and John Power

BRENT LIBRARIES	
KIN	
91120000391757	
Askews & Holts	11-Jan-2019
AF	£8.99

CONTENTS

SUMMER 1976

I've been thinking about my mother, and the summer I lied about Nisse Hofmann. For six long weeks the weather had been sweltering; you could be outside all day and never feel a breeze. I was turning eleven in September, but the hot days passed so slowly it felt like my birthday would never arrive. The birch tree on the lawn outside our apartment block stood still as a sentry; not a branch moved. Its bark grew dusty, and its leaves hung like rags. During the day, when there was no one else around, it was like the world had stopped.

In spring Mum and I had moved from Stockholm to this new estate outside the city. Everything was spotless and uniform, right down to the birch on the lawn outside each building. Lots of people wanted to live there, but Mum's boyfriend Anders knew someone at the housing company. It was Anders who had said we should leave our old place, because it was small and it was falling apart. He said this was the way to live: with room to move and green space around you. What only occurred to me later was that he didn't like the old apartment because Mum had lived there with my dad. And with me, but Dad had died a long time before, when I was too young to remember anything. 'He was fine and then he got sick and then he died,' is how Mum explained it. 'Just like that,' she said, clapping her hands together as if she was knocking flour from them. After we moved to the new place, away from my father's ghost, Anders tried calling me his little girl, but he didn't try for long.

#

Our building was long and rectangular and spectacularly white. It had four floors and four stairwells: A, B, C and D. We lived in 4B, on the second floor. On my bedroom wall I had a big poster map of the world and in my bedside drawer I kept a sheet of stickers, red and blue. The red stickers were for the countries I had been to, and the blue stickers were for countries I wanted to visit. The only countries with red stickers on them were Denmark and Sweden. Sometimes I took the sticker off Sweden because it felt like cheating, but sooner or later I always put it back. Over time the number of blue stickers grew: France, Ireland, Russia, Spain, Brazil, America, Yugoslavia. I picked countries because I liked the way their names sounded, or because I saw them on a television programme, or because I read about them in my mum's travel guide, a thick paperback I would heave into my lap and read for hours. Some, like Japan, I just liked the shape of.

Nisse Hofmann lived on the second floor too, one stairwell along. He was the same age as me, and he didn't have a dad either. Not only did our apartments neighbour each other, our bedrooms were right beside each other, too. I would see him at his window fixing stickers to the glass. From the outside you could only see their white backs, but from the shape of them I could tell they were soldiers and planes and cars. At night sometimes I would get out of bed and press my ear against the wall, trying to hear him.

Nisse's mum was the most beautiful woman I had ever seen. She had white-blonde hair and was so pretty that she looked cruel. I didn't understand how someone like her could exist in a place as boring as our apartment block. She seemed to be struggling with the same thought: I never once saw her look happy, but it didn't affect her beauty. My mum was pretty in her way, but the worry she always seemed to be feeling about one thing or another worked its way into the lines of her face and became the only thing you saw. I don't like looking in mirrors, but when I do it's her face that stares out at me. Except I'm much older now than she ever was.

When I saw Mrs Hofmann with different men I would wonder if they were as bad as Anders, or maybe even worse. In the night, now and then, I wondered if Nisse's

3

ear was ever pressed to the same patch of wall as mine, with just a few centimetres between us. I could see his blond hair glowing in the darkness of his room.

Not that I liked Nisse. He would tear around the apartment blocks like an animal, stamping on flowers and hitting the trees. He would soak a patch of dry earth and make the mud into discs he threw at other boys, then chase after girls with his black, slimy hands stretched out towards them. I kept myself away from those games. I played with other children from the estate sometimes, but not Nisse.

One day I saw a group of seven or eight children huddled over something at the corner of my block. They were standing and kneeling in the soil of a flowerbed, absorbed by something I couldn't see. Curious, I peered over their backs to find out what was so fascinating.

'What is it?' I asked, unable to see between their tightly packed bodies.

Just then Nisse, who had been hidden at the centre of the huddle, stood up, forcing everyone back. 'Only this,' he said as he turned and I saw a small blur rush towards me. Automatically I reached out to catch it: a dead mouse. It was only in my hands for a moment before I threw it to the ground, shuddering at the cold, rigid density of it, its fur spiky and sticky with dirt. The feel of it clung to my hands. Everyone around me was laughing.

'Dirty thing!' I screamed at Nisse.

I ran crying to my apartment, and eventually – when my mum had established I wasn't hurt in any way – I told her what had happened. 'Right,' she said, and left the apartment. I went to the window and watched her come out of our door and walk across to the next stairwell. That night I didn't need to put my ear to the wall: I could clearly hear Mrs Hofmann shouting at Nisse, although I couldn't make the hoarse, gruff voice I heard fit with her beauty. It was as if their apartment contained another woman who only appeared when someone had to be punished. Later, long after the shouting had stopped, I sat up in bed and pressed my ear to the cool wall. I remember smiling when I heard, very faintly, the sound of Nisse crying.

#

Mum worked in the office of a nearby factory, and Anders drove his elderly Saab into Stockholm every day to his job, which had something to do with the city's telephone lines. I asked him about it once and he told me it was too complicated for little girls. I was alone a lot during the holidays, but I didn't mind. As long as I had books to read I was never bored. During the day I often read in the spotty shade under the birch tree, moving around its trunk as its shadow moved across the lawn. It was like sitting

5

at the centre of a giant clock-face, the tree's shadow first sweeping along the length of our apartment block, then the neighbouring blocks. A couple of days after throwing the dead mouse at me, Nisse started running past. He pretended to ignore me, but I saw the little darting movements his eyes made, watching me sidelong. I was much better than him at disguising where I was looking. He was making loud noises and diving on the ground – storming machine-gun nests and throwing himself on grenades – but after a while he tired of this game and grew quiet. Absorbed in my book, the next time I looked up I was surprised to find him still there, staring up at our building.

'What will you give me if I get it through the middle window?' he said, holding up a red apple with a bite taken out of it.

He was looking at the landing windows, which stood open all day and all night that summer in an attempt to get some air circulating through the building.

'That's the window outside my apartment,' I said.

'I know. We're neighbours.'

My face got hot when he said that. Somehow I hadn't thought of the idea occurring to Nisse, or to anyone other than me. Maybe he really did put his ear to the wall like I did, I thought. Maybe each of us really had listened for the other at the same time. 'You'll miss,' I said.

'I won't.'

'OK then, prove you can do it.'

'But what will you give me?' Nisse said. He was trying to sound defiant, but there was a whine in his voice. It made me realise I had power over him. The thought excited me.

'Show me you can do it first,' I said offhandedly. 'Then we'll see.'

Nisse looked up at the window. He took a few steps back and bobbed the apple up and down a couple of times. As his right arm went back he held his left out in front of him, pointing straight up towards his target. He threw the apple hard, and it flew in through the open window like it had been jerked up there on a piece of string. It hit with a faint smack. Nisse turned around, grinning. I was grinning too.

'Told you,' he said. 'Now what do I get?'

I put my book on the ground beside me and stood up.

'Come here,' I said.

As Nisse walked towards me I felt gooseflesh wrinkle my skin, even in the heat of the day. He stood in front of me. We were the same height.

'Close your eyes,' I said.

'Why?'

'Close your eyes and you'll get your reward.'

Nisse closed his eyes and I put my hands on his shoulders. He flinched a little at my touch.

7

'Keep your eyes closed,' I said. He screwed them shut more tightly. I brought my lips to his. I closed my eyes as well, and felt a wave of something go through me. It was like running into a cold sea on a hot day.

We stayed like that for a few seconds, still as the tree above us. Then Nisse pulled back. He looked shocked. He tried to say something but only made a noise. He wiped his hand across his mouth then shoved me, and I fell backwards onto the dry grass. He ran away, disappearing around the corner of the building.

I didn't cry. I don't think I even wanted to. I felt a strange numbness as I looked at the ragged leaves hanging above me. I picked up my book and walked upstairs to the apartment. The apple had hit the wall of the landing outside our front door. It had exploded: a stain like thrown paint was visible on the wall, and white fragments of flesh had stuck there, and sprayed across the floor. They were already starting to brown in the heat. I stepped over them and let myself in, went straight to my room and lay down on the bed.

I heard Anders shouting as soon as he saw what Nisse had done. 'Vandals!' he yelled. He burst into my room, eyes alight, and asked what I knew about 'that disgusting mess at our front door'. I told him I'd been asleep all afternoon; that I didn't know anything about it. To my surprise, he believed me.

#

Mum and Anders liked to throw parties, especially that summer. They were good hosts, I suppose, because a lot of people came. The whole apartment filled with smoke and chatter, and empty glasses and bottles sprang up like weeds on tables, on the floor, on the bookshelves.

The music was always jazz, and in the morning Anders's records would be stacked in piles on top of the stereo speakers like big rounds of liquorice. Finding the right sleeve for each record gave me a feeling of immense satisfaction, and I loved studying the covers. Sometimes they showed the musician, and sometimes they depicted the album title. I remember one called *Cool Struttin'* that showed a woman in heels walking along a city street. But the ones I liked best had a more mysterious connection with the music: a small sailing boat on a grey sea, sunlight falling through a broken window, a sand dune in the desert. I loved to spread the albums on the floor around me and get lost in the pictures.

Mum would put me to bed later than usual on party nights, but still I found it hard to go to sleep. The heat made it difficult enough, but really it was hearing the voices and the music, and wanting more than anything to be there, in the middle of it. At one of the first parties that summer I remember creeping to my door and opening it a crack. The bedrooms were down a short hallway leading off the living room, which I could see a strip of from my doorway. Within that narrow space I saw people drinking and smoking and dancing.

It was a magical feeling, like watching a play from the side of the stage. That world seemed so special to me then, and all those people so sophisticated. But then you grow up, and you realise that special world, the one glimpsed through that doorway, isn't what you thought it was. It never really existed the way you imagined it to.

But leaning there that night, cheek pressed dozily to the doorframe, I saw something extraordinary: Mrs Hofmann, standing right there against the wall of our living room as if it were a cinema screen and she was projected onto it. Her hair was cut in a fringe that framed her beautiful face. She wore a denim dress with a bronze zip running from collar to hem, and brown leather boots. The man beside her had a mop of black hair and a scruffy brown suit. Was she really here with him? He looked like anyone. They were holding drinks and cigarettes and neither of them was talking, not to each other and not to anyone else. Then Mrs Hofmann moved out of my limited field of vision. The man remained for a few moments, gazing down into his glass. Then he followed her.

Thrilled at the sight of Mrs Hofmann in my home, and wanting to look at her for as long as possible, I crept out of my room and down the dim hallway towards the low orange light of the living room. The music from the stereo was very loud: a trumpet and the hectic clatter of drums. It reverberated in the hallway together with what sounded like a hundred shouting voices. There were probably only twenty people there, but it felt like a horde, and I knew, as I looked into the living room, that the night had reached some kind of peak. Nearly everybody was shouting or laughing. Some people were dancing wildly, shaking their heads to the trumpet blasts with sheens of sweat on their faces. Three men stood close together in intense discussion around the stereo, each gripping a record. I couldn't see Mum or Anders but I wasn't alarmed, the mood in the room was too happy to be worried about anything. Everyone was celebrating, or almost everyone. There on the couch, beside a man and woman kissing, sat Mrs Hofmann and her companion. Still and silent, they looked like they were waiting for the last bus on a cold night.

I woke up back in bed. Mum was sitting by my feet smoking a cigarette. The apartment was quiet. I shifted position, expecting her to turn, but she didn't react at all. I watched her face in the light from the sodium lamps on the neighbouring buildings, the ones that stayed on all night. She was almost expressionless, eyes staring. I decided she was thinking about Dad, or talking to him even. Letting him know how we were.

Those rare times we would talk about it she would only say it had all happened a long time ago, and that he loved me from up in heaven; then she would change the subject. She had a picture of him that she showed me, but only sparingly. I was so excited when she let me look at it, but I never asked her to; it seemed right that I shouldn't be able to see it whenever I wanted. It needed to be earned, albeit through some mysterious process I didn't understand.

When Mum died I expected to find more pictures of Dad in her things, but it really was the only one. I don't have it any more, but I can still remember every detail: black and white with a thin white border, unframed, and with a crease running across the top. Dad was sitting cross-legged on a jetty, bare-chested, wearing shorts and white plimsolls, squinting into the sun with one of those smiles that looks like pain. The smooth, black water behind him looked deep. I don't have any pictures of her, either.

The next day, after the party, it seemed wrong to ask Mum what she had been thinking about when she was sitting on my bed. It felt like something that would lose its power if we spoke about it. And then later, when she was diagnosed with cancer, of course it was forgotten. You think when death is approaching you'll get to ask all the big questions and tie up all the loose ends, but it wasn't like that for us. Mum went so quickly from being fine to being in great pain, and the medicine they gave her made her so sick. She was there, but she was veiled. When we were able to talk we talked about very ordinary things, things you don't remember afterwards. I wish I could remember just one of those conversations now.

#

Summer burned on. There were more parties, but if Mrs Hofmann came to them I didn't see her. Mum took me into Stockholm to get things for the new school year: exercise books, a pencil case, gym kit. She liked to do it early, weeks before anyone else. She worried that if she waited until later everything would be gone. I saw Nisse from time to time but we didn't speak, passing each other without comment or acknowledgement. He played war with the other boys, and devised unpleasant fates for insects he plucked from the flowerbeds, and ran around the buildings hitting the walls with sticks, while I sat and read: book after book, day after day.

Then several days passed during which I didn't see anyone. It seemed Nisse and the others had decided, for whatever reason, to play elsewhere. The lawn became my private kingdom. I was sitting there one day, in luxurious isolation, when a man approached me. It was Mr Fisk, the estate superintendent. He was a fat old man who spent most of his time smoking cigarettes and drinking brown bottles of beer in his cubbyhole.

'Little girl,' he said, 'can I ask you a question?'

I looked up at him. His square glasses shone with sunlight, white blocks that hid his eyes. He knelt down in front of me. He smelled like the apartment after a party, a complex and intriguingly adult smell.

'What's your name?' he said.

'Eva.'

'Eva, that's right. You're Marie and Anders's little girl.'

'Marie Jönsson is my mum,' I said. 'Anders Hedlund is *not* my dad.'

Mr Fisk apologised, and at the time I thought he meant it, but he was probably just amused by this irritable little girl. He asked me if I liked living on the estate, then asked if I spent much time around the building – on the lawn where we were now, for example. I nodded, nervous about where his questions were leading.

'Who else plays here?' Mr Fisk said.

'Lots of people. I need to go now,' I said, but before I could get up he put his hand on my arm.

'Have you seen anyone doing anything they shouldn't? Have you seen anyone throwing things at the building?'

I didn't say anything.

'The Lindebloms have been away for the last few days and they've come home to a horrible mess: lumps of rotting fruit outside their door. Flies. Wasps. They're very upset.'

The Lindeblooms' apartment was on the top floor of our stairwell. I was impressed Nisse had managed to get anything all the way up there. I felt warmly towards him then, and for a moment I thought of telling Mr Fisk that it was Anders. That every day after dinner Anders would come down onto the lawn with an apple and toss it up through the stairwell window for fun. I saw Mr Fisk marching Anders out of the building, his hands bound like a criminal. But I knew he wouldn't believe me, so I told him the truth. 'It was Nisse,' I said.

'Nisse?'

'Nisse Hofmann.'

'Nisse Hofmann? Are you sure?'

'Yes,' I said, moving away from him. 'Nisse does it all the time.' I ran away. As I reached the door of the stairwell I turned back to see him still crouched by the tree, staring after me like a simpleton. I hated him.

'Nisse did it!' I shouted, and turned and ran upstairs.

#

That night I lay in bed waiting for Mrs Hofmann to start shouting. I wondered if I would get in trouble too. I felt like throwing up. Outside my window I heard a dustbin lid clatter to the ground, and the answering bark of a dog.

15

Like every other night of that summer, the air in my room stood thick as jam. It was too dark to make out the countries on my map, but I could see the black lumps of the continents: Europe, Africa, the Americas. As I looked at them, they appeared to grow in the darkness. I stood on my bed and put my ear to the smooth wall. I squeezed my eyes shut and concentrated as hard as I could on hearing something, but I could only hear myself: the blood hissing in my veins, the treacherous words blocking up my throat.

#

I never even considered the possibility that it wasn't Nisse who smashed the fruit outside the Lindeblooms' apartment, but the day after he spoke to me Mr Fisk knocked on our door. We had just sat down to dinner. Anders was complaining, about traffic or politicians or the idiots he was surrounded by at work, like he did every evening. I wasn't listening; all I could think about was the summer ending and school beginning. I got so used to my own company in the holidays that it was difficult to be around so many people again. Mum, too, was somewhere else entirely. You could taste her distraction in the burned meat and hard potatoes.

'Can I speak to your parents, Eva?' Mr Fisk said when I opened the door. He sat down with us at the dinner table, declined food, accepted beer, and asked Mum and Anders if I had told them about 'our little chat' the day before.

'She hasn't,' Anders said, and frowned at me, an expression that triggered a spurt of fear.

Mr Fisk explained what we had talked about, and described what the Lindebloms had found when they came back from their trip. 'And it's not just this block,' he said. 'This has been happening all over. Potatoes, cabbages, apples – sometimes stones. Someone's been very busy.'

'It happened here!' Anders said. 'People are pigs.' He stabbed the table's oilcloth cover with his finger. 'You give them a nice place to live and they muck it up.'

'Anders,' Mum said. He lit a cigarette and pushed his plate away from him.

Mum looked at me, then at Mr Fisk. 'Surely you don't think it was Eva . . . ?' she said.

'No, no! I just wanted to ask her again about what she told me. It was a little confusing and I wanted to be sure.'

'What did you tell Mr Fisk, Eva?' Mum said, leaning towards me.

I looked at the potatoes on my plate.

'What's this silent act?' Anders said. 'Speak up, Eva, answer your mother.'

I couldn't speak. I couldn't say again what I had said before.

'She told me it was Nisse Hofmann,' said Mr Fisk.

'Oh,' Mum said. She sounded sad to hear it.

Anders snorted, as if he had known all along. 'She lets him run wild,' he said. He leaned conspiratorially towards Mr Fisk. 'You know, she—' he began, but Mum cut him off.

'"She" has had a hard time, Anders, as you know. So enough.' She didn't sound tired now. Her voice was steady and strong.

Anders shrugged and slumped back in his chair. He flicked sulkily at a tear in the oilcloth, like a child. There was a pause.

'It's just I haven't seen them around,' Mr Fisk said, clearly uncomfortable about whatever was passing between Mum and Anders. 'Most people tell me when they're going away so I can keep an eye on things for them, but Mrs Hofmann – never. I can't say for sure, but they're never in when I go round and no one's seen them. So I just wanted to ask Eva,' here he turned to me and took extra care to pronounce each word, 'if she was absolutely sure that she saw Nisse doing what she said.'

They all looked at me and waited for my answer: fat Mr Fisk; sulky Anders; my anxious mum, with sorrow contorting her face.

\#

That night I woke to find Mum sitting at the end of my bed. The light from the lamps outside shone on the tip of her nose and her eye, which was the only part of her that was moving. A cigarette burned between her fingers but she didn't raise it to her mouth.

'Mum?' I whispered. 'Mum!'

But either she didn't hear me or she didn't want to answer. I fell back asleep, and when I woke up again she was gone.

\#

Two days later Mrs Hofmann came to our apartment. It was just after nine at night. I was curled up in a chair, reading. Anders was watching something about the election on TV – it was going to happen on my birthday. Mum was at the kitchen table looking at photographs taken when I was a baby. Every so often she would say my name, and when I looked over she would be holding up a picture of me looking fat and startled.

'This is when you were eight months old,' she said. Then, 'This was at your Uncle Kalle's house.' Then, 'You loved those little shoes so much. You cried when they didn't fit any more.'

All the pictures looked exactly the same to me.

The bell rang, and Mrs Hofmann was speaking before

Mum had the door all the way open. Her words came fast and venomous. Blood surged into my face and I felt like I was shivering. I wanted to run to my room and climb out of the window, but found myself standing up and moving to where I could see the front door.

Mum invited Mrs Hofmann in, but she refused. 'Two weeks away,' she said, 'and I return to this note, this note full of lies about Nisse. How did he do all this from Gothenburg?' she said, waving a piece of paper in Mum's face. 'Please tell me how.'

Mrs Hofmann's voice grew louder and louder as she went on. I could see Nisse standing beside her. He was looking right at me, but was expressionless as if I wasn't there.

I felt two hands press down on my shoulders and Anders frogmarched me to the door. Mrs Hofmann pointed her finger at me and said, 'Her. That one. She has been lying about my son.'

I expected Mum to say something, to tell Mrs Hofmann not to talk to me like that, but she only looked at me sorrowfully. She still had a photograph of me in her hand.

Then Anders was talking, but I didn't listen to what he said. I looked at Nisse, who continued to stare right through me. Mrs Hofmann and Anders talked for a long time. At one point he shook me by the shoulders and told me to say I was sorry, and I did. They agreed that I'd go with Mrs Hofmann the next day and explain everything to Mr Fisk. I didn't tell them I really had seen Nisse throw an apple through the window. I didn't tell them anything at all.

Late that night, as I was drifting off to sleep, I thought I heard tapping through the wall. The sound was coming from Nisse's bedroom. I lay there waiting to hear it again, deciding whether or not to tap back. I was still trying to decide when I fell asleep.

#

It was already hot when I pressed the buzzer to the Hofmanns' apartment the next morning. It had been warm even when Mum came into my room before she left for work, the sky still getting light. She told me she was very disappointed. Just that, nothing else. It was more than Anders managed. He only stood silently in my doorway for a few seconds before stomping off and slamming the front door.

As soon as I pressed the buzzer I heard Mrs Hofmann coming down the stairs. She had obviously been waiting for me. I saw her through the glass of the stairwell door, wearing a white dress and brown leather sandals. She looked like she should have been descending into the lobby of some grand hotel in Paris, not a concrete stairwell in a Stockholm suburb. I remembered Mum's tired face looking down on me in bed that morning. That, I thought, was the face of a woman who belonged here.

Mrs Hofmann opened the door and Nisse followed her out, dressed in a clean white shirt, black shorts and polished black shoes. I'd never seen him look so smart. I had picked what I was wearing off the floor, and my jeans had grass-stained knees. None of us spoke on the way to Mr Fisk's cubbyhole. The chattering birdsong falling from the trees seemed like mockery. All I wanted to do was get this over with, pick up a book and disappear again. I looked at the ground, and at Mrs Hofmann's slim legs moving ahead of me. She held Nisse's hand as he stamped along the path. But why was no one holding my hand? I can still feel, fifty years later, the absolute loneliness of that walk, perhaps more strongly, even, than I felt it then. Then I thought I was above everything, that nothing could touch me. Who was she, I thought, this glamorous woman stuck in the suburbs? And this silly boy she was raising, who, if he wasn't guilty of this, was certainly guilty of something. But when I stood in that musty room, when I looked at Mr Fisk and told him I was sorry for telling a lie, I found that I couldn't stop myself crying. And when I cried, it was my mum's anxious face I saw and that only made it worse. But I didn't cry because I had disappointed her. I was crying *for* her, and because of where she was: with stupid Anders and their stupid parties. And I was crying for Mrs Hofmann, who didn't want to be here at all, and for Nisse, who was just a silly boy without a father, and of course for me, too, most of all for me. I cried so much that Mrs Hofmann put a stiff hand on my shoulder and rubbed it to try and calm me down.

#

On the weekend before I went back to school, Mum and Anders threw the last party of the summer. All day the sky had been growing darker, and by dusk the distant grumble of thunder could be heard. The evening air was greasy with the coming storm.

The music was so loud there was no question of sleeping, and I lay awake in bed until the rain started. When it came down it sounded like sizzling fat. I went to the open window to watch: the drooping leaves of the birch were moving, for the first time in what felt like years. Drops of rain bounced up from the sill onto my face and chest. The water was cool, the air fresh. I heard screams and applause coming from the living room. For the rain? I went to my bedroom door but all I saw was a confusing jumble of parts of people, so I crept down the hallway to get a better view. I didn't need to creep at all: it was a cacophony. The windows were thrown open to the pouring skies, and the roar of the rain blended with the watery rush of cymbals while drums beat frantically under buzzing lines of saxophone and trumpet. The cheering continued; each time it seemed to be coming to an end it caught again and grew louder. The lights were low, lower than usual, and everyone was dancing, moving together in the too-small living room. I saw a man squatting like a toad at the feet of a woman, shaking his head and grimacing. The woman's hands moved in her hair as she jerked her head violently from side to side. A man was turning a circle with a woman held in his arms, her legs clamped around his waist and her hands waving. Another man danced alone, jabbing his fingers at the air and shouting, 'Yes! Yes!' in time with the music. Through the mass of bodies I saw Mum on the other side of the room. Her eyes were closed and her head turned up to the ceiling. The first few buttons of her shirt were undone and the lace of her bra was showing. Anders was directly behind her, his hands gripping her hips. As I watched, her eyes flew open and fixed on a point just above my head. All their dulling sorrow had been washed away. They blazed. In that moment she was more beautiful even than Mrs Hofmann.

She was alive for another two years, but I never saw that look on her face again. It comes back to me still, on nights when I can't sleep. Who was she really, this woman? She was my mum, of course, but that was only one

part, and I want to know all the parts. I could have asked
Anders, but I have no idea what happened to him, and I
don't think he would have been able to tell me. Not the
way that man on the jetty could tell me. So I don't ask; I
remember. Remember and imagine. I imagine her sitting
on the edge of my bed, her face outlined in the glow of
lamps that burn, if they still burn at all, hundreds of kilometres from where I sit writing this. A forgotten cigarette
shrinks between her fingers. She stares out of the window,
but what she is looking at I cannot see.

ABOVE THE WEDDING

'Can you be here a week before the wedding, Cameron?'
Nuria's voice crumpled as the Skype connection failed:
her frozen face pixelated. She hung there waiting for an
answer, Mexico City a rain-marked window behind her. It
was a hot summer evening in Brixton. Huddled together
in front of the laptop screen, Liam and Cameron's arms
stuck lightly where they touched.

'We're there,' Cameron said.

Nuria's face remained static.

'We'll be there,' Liam echoed, unsure she could hear
what they were saying.

She unfroze mid-sentence: '. . . say you're both coming?'

'Yeah,' Cameron said, leaning closer to the screen. 'Li's
coming too.'

'Oh,' she said. 'That's great.'

Cameron and Nuria had met three years before, on
a ferry between Greek islands. She had recently moved
to Barcelona from Mexico to study, and Cameron was
spending the summer helping renovate a friend's house
on Naxos. That autumn, when Cameron returned to

London, he and Liam moved in together. It had been their parents' idea, something Liam wasn't supposed to know. They thought Cameron – younger by fourteen months, but always the more sensible brother – could get him 'back on an even keel', the phrase Liam could practically hear his mother saying when Cameron, drunk one night, admitted the whole arrangement.

Liam met Nuria when she came to see Cameron in London. She brought her boyfriend, Miguel. On the Saturday night of their visit they went out with a large group of Cameron's friends, and Liam tagged along. There was a lot of drink and some cocaine, and they ended up at a party in a mazelike warehouse in Shadwell. Liam and Miguel lost the others and tried calling Cameron and Nuria, but no one had reception. It was around three when Miguel suggested leaving. On the cab ride to Brixton they talked about the differences between growing up in London and Barcelona. They were both yawning as they got in, but decided on another drink. They were in the flat's cramped kitchen, talking about Spanish football, when it happened. Miguel pressed close into Liam and started kissing him, moving against him with a violent energy. Liam, who had never kissed a man before, kissed Miguel back. They moved to Liam's bedroom, but Liam's phone rang before anything could happen.

'Where are you?' said Cameron.

Liam heard the nervousness that edged the question. He heard people laughing in the background. 'We're at home,' he said.

'Miguel's with you?' Relief slid into Cameron's voice.

'Yeah, he's right here.' Miguel was sitting still on the edge of the bed, his shirt and jeans open.

'Miguel's there,' Liam heard Cameron say.

'Mi amor!' Nuria shouted. Three or four other voices repeated the phrase.

'We'll be home soon, Li,' Cameron said. 'There's a few of us. We're picking up booze.' Cameron said something away from the mouthpiece, then his voice returned. 'Liam . . .'

'Yes?'

'It was good tonight, wasn't it?'

Liam knew what the question really meant. 'Don't be a headcase. Don't be a fucking weirdo.' 'Yeah,' he said, 'I had a great time.'

'And you're OK?'

'I'm good, Cam. See you in a bit.' He ended the call and looked at Miguel, who was looking at the floor. 'They're on their way.'

'This did not happen,' Miguel said.

#

29

In the weeks after the visit, when he saw an opportunity, Liam steered conversations around to Miguel. He was a web developer, Cameron told him. He worked freelance and was often away from Nuria and Barcelona, which gave Liam a thrill of pleasure to hear. The more time that passed, the more Liam found himself playing out what might have happened that night if Cameron had called twenty minutes later.

'You guys really got on, didn't you?' Cameron said, after another of Liam's questions.

He shrugged. 'Seems like a good guy.'

#

Nuria invited Cameron to Nice, where Miguel was working, and Cameron suggested Liam join them. Liam, buried under several years' worth of credit-card debt, said he couldn't afford it, but Cameron offered to pay. 'Come on, they'd love to see you again.'

'I don't know,' Liam said, scraping a foil container of takeaway noodles onto two plates.

'What are you going to do otherwise?'

'Sit there,' Liam said, nodding through the kitchen doorway at the couch. 'Soil myself.'

'You're not funny, Li.'

'Oh yeah I am. Bone-cancer funny.'

Cameron gave him nothing.

Liam sighed. 'Maybe I should get back to the book,' he said. 'Really get stuck into it.' A couple of years before Liam had started writing a novel, although it hadn't got beyond a page of bullet points and a few disconnected scenes.

'You say that, Liam,' said Cameron, 'and it would be great if you did, but you'll probably end up doing something . . . less productive. Come to Nice. Get me back whenever.'

Liam saw himself beside the water with Miguel, under an empty blue sky. They were the only two people on the beach. He handed Cameron a plate. 'Eat your noodles,' he said.

#

On their second night in Nice they went out with a big group of Miguel's workmates: Americans, Belgians, Germans, Slovakians. By midnight everyone was very drunk. At the last bar, Moby Dick's, rounds of shots were ordered. Liam felt the alcohol charging through him. Miguel raised a pack of cigarettes in his direction and tilted his head towards the door. They went outside. It was the first time they had been alone that weekend. They stood away from the other smokers, a little way down the otherwise quiet side street.

'So I wanted to email you,' Liam said, 'but I didn't know if I should, or if you'd want me to.'

Miguel looked past Liam, back to the bar. He balled his hand into a fist, raised it to his head and knocked it against his temple, then grasped Liam's arm and pulled. They jogged down the street, their shoulders bumping. Liam looked at Miguel, but Miguel only looked ahead. A pace behind Miguel, Liam crossed the broad, empty road that followed the seafront. They climbed over the promenade railings and dropped down onto the pebbles. The streetlights illuminated a band of the empty beach, and beyond it Liam saw a ragged white line where small waves were breaking. At the base of the promenade wall, where they stood, no light fell. Miguel turned Liam around and pushed him up against the wall, its stone sharp against his chest. Miguel's hands worked urgently, popping open the buttons of Liam's jeans. He tugged them down roughly. He used his foot to push Liam's legs apart, and yanked his hips backwards. Liam felt a sharp, hot pain and pressed his palms against the stone. He cried out and pulled away, shaking his head. Miguel turned him around, knelt in the sand and took him in his mouth. Liam stood frozen in the wall's dense shadow, the hiss of the sea before him and cars sweeping past on the road above. It had never felt like this. He knew he would never forget the way it felt.

#

Liam wrote to Miguel after Nice, cutting and pasting his address from a group email, but there was no reply. A month later, Cameron told him Miguel and Nuria were getting married. Liam saw Miguel once more after the wedding announcement, after Nuria contacted him to suggest a surprise trip to Berlin for Cameron's birthday.

At a club that had once been a power plant, Liam and Miguel wandered off separately then found each other again. They hid themselves in the corner of a dark side room. Miguel was fast, rough. He pressed Liam against the wall and pushed himself inside him. Liam moaned loudly, unable to stay silent. The pain of it, excruciating at first, was swallowed by something larger: a numbness that grew into a boiling joy. He felt Miguel's hands on him. He felt the wall's cool brick under his hands. Afterwards they kissed, Liam angling his face down towards Miguel's.

'I really like you,' Liam whispered into Miguel's ear. Miguel smiled and pressed his palms against Liam's face.

'You are a good guy,' Miguel said, butting his forehead against Liam's.

Liam had planned to ask Miguel about the wedding, if it was what he really wanted, but at that moment it was the last thing he wanted to talk about.

\#

After Berlin Liam emailed Miguel a second time, a couple of lines saying how much he had enjoyed it, and that he wanted to talk. Maybe Skype? Nothing came back. As the date of the wedding approached Liam wondered if he should go, the thought of it filling him with fear and eagerness. It must mean something, he thought, that he had been invited at all. Sick of trying and failing to not think about Miguel, Liam headed for Soho on a mild midsummer night with the intention of going with another man. Alone on the upper deck, as the bus jounced over potholes, he let himself imagine this was the first night of a new life. Before Miguel there had been nothing like this, but maybe he had always wanted it.

He walked into the first place he came to on Old Compton Street and sat at the bar with a drink. To his surprise, it wasn't long before someone was talking to him. Posh. Blond. Handsome. He said his name was William. 'Or Will, if you like.'

'The best Will in the world,' Liam said. He was nervous and knew he sounded foolish, but Will laughed – surprising Liam again – and after that the conversation was easy: jobs; music; travel; food. They had another drink, then another. Will asked Liam if he wanted to get some fresh air.

They walked up Greek Street, past tides of smokers washed from the bars and restaurants. At the top of the street Soho Square lay in darkness, hemmed in by partly lit buildings. Will gripped Liam's shoulder.

'Shall we go in?' he said. 'I know where we can squeeze through.'

Liam nodded. His mouth was too dry to speak. The light from the nearest lamp post fell at an angle and cut Will's face in two, silver and black. They walked along the narrow pavement between parked cars and the spiked railings that ran around the square. At one corner, in a patch of shadow, a single railing was bent in a shallow V. It looked like a raised eyebrow, which made Liam smile. Will slipped through the fence and he followed.

In the darkness Liam focused on Will's blond hair, its faint glow like a clouded moon. What was happening, what was about to happen, seemed unreal. They stopped. Will turned, smiled, said, 'Come here,' and cupped Liam's jaw in his hands. His tongue was hot, large, searching. It pushed, hard, to the back of Liam's mouth. Liam's tongue answered, pushing back, but Will's did not give. Will moved his hand to Liam's groin and, finding no erection, started rubbing the heel of his hand up and down, up and down. Liam pulled his head back and Will followed, laughing lightly, keeping his mouth locked onto Liam's. With Miguel it was like they adhered to one another, but

35

his body and Will's were at war. Will's tongue filled Liam's mouth greedily, sloppily. There was too much of him. He took Will's shoulders and pushed. He backed off and Will reached for him, but Liam knocked his hand away.

'Fucking cock tease.'

Liam stopped going out after that. It wasn't because he had spent all his money on a ticket for Mexico – he could always run up more debt. But after his encounter with Will an old feeling returned: a curtain that separated him from the rest of the world.

Cameron noticed the change. 'I don't like you spending so much time alone,' he said one night, after coming home to find Liam asleep with a scatter of beer cans around him, his body slid halfway off the couch. 'You want some shifts at my place?' Cameron managed a venue that hosted corporate events.

'Don't worry about me,' Liam said, dazed from beer and sleep, 'this is my me-time.'

Liam had a job, at a second-hand bookshop five minutes from the flat, that made few demands of him. He was having his first drink earlier and earlier in the day. He had made an attempt to write, but didn't get further than opening the Word document, last modified two years earlier, and scanning it for five minutes before closing it again. In his memory there had been more, and it had been better.

A month before the wedding he broke his self-imposed ban and went on Nuria's Facebook page looking for pictures of Miguel. He saw him beside Nuria, standing in front of a table filled with gifts. Miguel's right arm ran around Nuria's back, his hand cupping her hip, her hand resting on his. His left hand was placed delicately on her waist. Liam scrolled down further, past pictures of Nuria hugging her friends, news stories, cartoons, quotations, GIFs. He scrolled faster then stopped, moved back up the page. Here was Miguel standing in the ocean, white garlands of foam around his shins. He was wearing cut-off jeans and his brown belly was taut, his hands stretched up over his head. Liam felt the stone of the promenade wall against his chest. The angle at which the picture had been taken made it look like Miguel was holding the sun's white, blurred circle between his hands. By the time Liam arrived in Mexico it would be more than a year since Berlin. Nothing will happen, he told himself. Something will happen.

#

Because Miguel and Nuria had friends coming from so far away – from Europe, South America, the US – they had planned a week of activities leading up to the wedding. The first of these was getting together all the overseas guests, and some of Nuria's oldest friends from Mexico City, at a rented villa in Acapulco.

When Liam and Cameron left London there had been ice on the ground, but here the temperature was in the mid-twenties. On the beach, his back to the ocean, Liam looked at the white hotel towers and apartment blocks standing along the shoreline. He was drinking a mixture of beer, spiced tomato juice and clam broth that had been recommended to him by a couple of Nuria's friends as the best thing for a hangover. People lay scattered on loungers beneath a mushroom-like cluster of sunshades, one or two making occasional trips to the water. The previous night had been long and loud, and although Liam had been last to bed, in the blue light of dawn, he was sure some other people must feel as bad as he did.

They had been at a club on a cliff above the city. At some point Cameron had talked Nuria into teaching Liam to dance. 'He doesn't want to,' she said, smiling and shaking her head, but Cameron kept insisting until she stood and held her hand out above the drinks crowding the table.

'You have to move these,' Nuria shouted above the stamping beat, rotating Liam's rigid hips with her hands. The club was busy but the dancefloor was sparsely populated, and Liam felt embarrassed by this public lesson. Nuria took his hands, put them on her hips and rested her wrists on his shoulders. She undulated casually and her straight black hair swung behind her. She stared at his waist and smiled at what she saw. A few men danced closer, looking at Nuria. Liam thought of her moving like this with Miguel, and the thought brought Miguel closer to him. He wanted Nuria to look at him the way she looked at Miguel, to be able, for a moment, to see what Miguel saw. His hand on Nuria's hip made him think of the photograph he'd seen, of Miguel's hand cupping it. He tightened his grip on Nuria's hips and tried to make the same flowing movements with his own. It was like fucking, the way she was moving. 'Good,' she said, but when he looked up her expression – although it was hard to be sure as the lights flickered across her face – seemed taunting. He couldn't move the way she moved, and he laughed to distract her from his staccato thrusting. She pulled him close, her fingernails digging painfully into his neck. 'You have to let go,' she said.

Liam pulled away, shrugging an apology. 'English hips!' he shouted above the music, backing off the dancefloor. Nuria flicked her hand dismissively and continued to dance. Liam touched his neck, feeling the indentations left by her nails. Then Cameron cannoned into him, a bottle of tequila in his hand, and he didn't remember a lot after that.

On their last day in Acapulco they took a trip on a glass-bottomed cruise boat. They crossed the bay, and at the foot of a cliff the engines were cut. Everyone crowded onto the top deck to watch a cliff diver. Only Liam stayed below. He hoped Miguel would notice and take the opportunity to join him; since he had arrived they had only exchanged a few pleasantries. Liam, hungover again, his mouth gritty and his head throbbing queasily, listened to the guide's loud voice, distorted by the boat's tannoy. The man repeated the words 'Click-click camera' over and over, like a prayer.

Because of the narrow view available from the lower deck Liam couldn't see the diver, only a sandy strip of cliff with green waves curling at its base. After what seemed like a long time he heard cheers and saw a small splash, followed by a bigger cheer. He saw the diver in the water, waving at the boat. He saw Miguel coming down to the lower deck and he tensed in anticipation, then saw someone else behind him. Nuria. 'Here you are,' she said, sitting down beside Liam. Miguel waved vaguely and sat on her far side. 'How come you're not upstairs?'

'I burn,' Liam said, lifting and shaking his milk-white forearm.

'But your brother is up there.'

'He got all the good genes,' Liam said. He laughed, too loudly and for too long. Embarrassed, he cleared his throat and rubbed his face.

'This isn't the real place for cliff diving, anyway,' Nuria

said. 'That happens around the bay. La Quebrada. They dive at night with torches; they look like falling stars. It's super-touristic, but I think it's impressive, anyway.'

Liam nodded, and then Nuria placed her hand on his arm, gently but firmly, as if she were consoling him. Her hand radiated warmth. He smiled at her and looked past her at Miguel, who was flicking something from his shorts. Water slapped against the hull. Liam expected someone to say something, but no one did. The engines sputtered to life. People began to drift down to the lower deck, and Nuria stood to answer someone's question about what was going to happen next.

Further out, where the bay opened into the ocean, the boat stopped again above a statue on the seabed. 'The Holy Virgin of Guadeloupe,' the guide intoned piously, his amplified voice crackling. Everyone crowded around the boat's glass bottom. It took Liam some time to work out what he was seeing in the cloudy turquoise water. A few metres down a woman stood on a weed-covered rock with her hands joined in prayer. Her upturned stone face was spattered with moss and clams. Her eyes were blank. The weeds waved slowly at her feet. If he was down there with her, Liam wondered, would the noise from this crowded boat reach him? She looked so lonely. A squadron of small silver fish sped to a halt beside her, paused, shot away. There had been a statue of Mary, Liam remembered, at his family's parish church when he was a child. Our Lady, they called her. Throughout the service, whichever pew he was fidgeting on that week, Liam always found his gaze being dragged back to her. She wore a blue cowl over a white robe, and her face was infinitely kind. She held one of her hands down by her hip, palm upward, and the other was raised at shoulder height, two fingers together as if she was holding an invisible cigarette. To her left, on the wall behind the altar, hung Jesus, his skin torn and his eyes rolled back in an agony that looked, the closer Liam got to sixteen and the announcement of his atheism, increasingly orgasmic. He felt again the hot surge of Miguel inside him, and the rough brick catching on his hands.

#

Liam and Cameron spent the days before the wedding in Mexico City. They stayed in Zona Rosa, Nuria and Miguel's neighbourhood, at the cheapest hostel they could find. One night Nuria's family held something called a posada at their house, a little way out of the city centre. 'We sing songs about Joseph and Mary coming to Bethlehem,' she explained. 'We eat a lot, drink a lot.' The garden was strung with lights, and a large cabana set with tables of food and drink. Nuria's parents gave a short welcome speech to their guests, including some sentences in English for the non-Spanish speakers. They were glamorous, her father tall and thin with a silver moustache, her mother big-featured: large lips, a prominent nose. The man and woman beside them, Liam realised, must be Miguel's parents. They were short and overweight, and beside the elegance of their hosts their clothes looked cheap.

The day had been warm but the nights were very cold, near freezing, and many of the guests clutched hot mugs of chocolate. Liam approached a table filled with bottles and poured a large measure of whiskey into his. After the singing, led enthusiastically by Nuria's mother, a piñata in the shape of a star was brought into the garden. One of Nuria's brothers scrambled onto a flat roof to hold one end of the rope it hung from, while the other used a tree branch as a pulley. Nuria went first. Blindfolded, she held the pole above her head like a samurai. She stepped forwards and backwards as the piñata dangled just above her, her head twitching as if in response to its movements. She raised one leg, karate style, but as everyone laughed at her clowning she struck, too quickly for her brothers to jerk the piñata away. Her blow tore through the papier-mâché, and sweets and toys and what looked like scratch cards gushed from the smashed star. Everyone cheered. Nuria laughed as she lifted her blindfold and held the pole in the air in triumph. The prizes glimmered at her feet.

Later, when he saw Miguel leaving, Liam followed him onto the dark driveway at the front of the house. He knew Nuria was staying with her parents until the wedding, and that Miguel was alone in their apartment. Here, as in Acapulco, Miguel had barely spoken a word to him. As the security light above the garage flicked on, frosting the driveway white, Liam called his name.

Miguel stopped, turned.

'You're going to have to talk to me some time,' Liam said.

Miguel smiled, not unkindly. 'No I am not, Liam,' he said, and turned and walked into the darkness.

After everyone else had gone, Nuria and Cameron stayed up late, sitting in the cold drinking vodka and re-telling old stories. Nuria, a thick blanket over her legs, had her feet in Cameron's lap. Liam was relieved when she suggested he go inside and find a couch to sleep on.

He was woken the next morning by Nuria's parents leaving the house: he heard them talking to her in the hallway. Her mother said something that made everyone laugh. Liam showered and found Cameron in the kitchen where the maid, a young woman called Xoco, fried them quesadillas for breakfast. Nuria said Xoco wanted to prac-tise her English, but when Liam said, 'Hello Xoco, how are you?' she only smiled at her shoes and shook her head.

A book about Aztecs lay on the kitchen table, and Liam flipped its pages as he ate. He saw photographs of stone serpents, ruined pyramids and blocky humanoid statues whose faces expressed pain and fury. He stopped at a picture of a brightly painted stone disc. Carved into the stone in low relief was the dismembered corpse of a woman, white bone jutting from her severed legs.

After breakfast Cameron went back to bed, and Liam and Nuria sat in the sunny garden. The family's beagle, Helecho, snarled and convulsed on the grass. He writhed on his back, the top of his head pressed into the ground; his eyes rolled and his paws hung limply in the air.

'He's showing off,' Nuria said, smiling at the dog. For a few minutes neither of them spoke. Sounds drifted from other houses: the banging of a pan, a lawnmower's drone. Xoco opened the kitchen door, dropped a bulging plastic bag into a bin and went back inside. Liam stood up, lit a cigarette, and wandered back and forth across the garden as he smoked. Helecho orbited him like a deranged moon, pounced on his shadow then streaked into a bush. The bush shook furiously.

'What was the carving in that book?' Liam said.

'What carving?'

'A woman with her arms and legs torn off. Wearing a big headdress.'

'Coyolxauhqui,' said Nuria.

'Coil . . . ?'

'Coyolxauhqui; an Aztec goddess. Her brother killed her. Huitzilopochtli, the god of war and the sun.'

'Why did he do that?'

Nuria, her eyes closed, tilted her head back so that her face caught the sun. 'Coyolxauhqui's mother was Coatlicue, the earth goddess. She was made pregnant by a ball of feathers.'

Liam laughed. 'A ball of feathers? Really?'

Nuria cocked open an eye, her head still tipped back. 'You want to hear it or not?'

'OK,' Liam said, his hands held up. 'OK, a ball of feathers. Of course.'

Nuria closed her eye. 'So Coatlicue got pregnant, but all her other sons and daughters thought she'd been . . .' – she waved her hand – 'sleeping around, you know?'

Liam nodded.

'So her daughter, Coyolxauhqui, came up with this plot to kill her. But as she and all her brothers – it was an army; Coatlicue had, like, hundreds of kids – as they got near the cave where their mother lived, Coatlicue gave birth to Huitzilopochtli. He came right out of the womb ready for battle, in armour, and he killed his sister and all her brothers ran away across the sky and became the stars. Then, because he saw Coatlicue was sad, he chopped off

46

Coyolxauhqui's head and threw it into the sky where it became the moon, so the mother could always see her daughter.'

'Her daughter's severed head.'

'Right. Sweet, no?'

Liam looked at Nuria, her eyes closed and her smiling face upturned to the morning sun. He liked her, and felt sorry for her. He wished there was some way to apologise. A tiny brown bird landed on the garden fence. Helecho sprang up, barking, and it flew away.

\#

The wedding was in the town of Cuautla, a couple of hours south of Mexico City. The night before the wedding, at the hotel where most of the guests were staying, there was a dinner for close friends and family, to which Cameron and Liam were invited. Liam knew his invitation was a matter of politeness. Cameron was in the bathroom getting ready, and Liam was sitting outside on a small brick patio that belonged to the room. He smoked a cigarette and gazed at the sunlit lawn stretching away from him, studded with small sprinklers. Unexpectedly, he saw a rabbit crouched in the shade of a low hedge, frozen except for its twitching nose. From somewhere out of sight he heard the hum of machinery, a hypnotic sound.

A hand gripped his shoulder and he jerked in his seat, his iron chair squealing against the brick.

'Jesus!' said Cameron, laughing. 'What the fuck is wrong with you these days?'

'Fuck's wrong with you?' Liam said, standing.

'Christ, Li, nothing,' Cameron snapped back. Then, anxiously, 'Are you OK?'

'That fucking tone, Cam, give it a rest. Yes, I'm OK. I'm OK.'

Cameron stepped closer, their chests touching. 'Fuck off, Li,' he hissed.

Liam's breath came fast, shallow. They hadn't fought physically since they were teenagers, but he wanted to lash out now. He slowed his breathing and forced a laugh. It wheezed out like air from a bike pump. 'You just surprised me, I'm sorry.' He brushed ash from his shirt. 'Look at this, Jesus,' he said, trying to get Cameron to smile, but he only turned and went back inside.

At dinner Nuria's father gave a speech that sounded very suave, although Liam had no idea what he was talking about. Miguel's father, who spoke next, was obviously nervous. Every few lines he would chuckle, but Liam didn't see anyone else finding what he had to say particularly funny. On the wall, throughout the dinner, a slideshow of photographs played: Miguel and Nuria as children, as teenagers, and together as adults. The pictures showed them on snowy mountains and at beach bars, around tables covered with food, in grey European streets and green forests; already a sprawling life together in a few short years. Liam recognised some of the pictures from Nuria's Facebook. Gulping wine, he looked at Miguel several tables away, leaning over to hear something his mother was saying. How could he talk to him? He wished he hadn't come.

After dinner Liam and Cameron joined a group going into Cuautla for a fiesta. The main street of the town was lined with people. Floats moved slowly down the centre of the street and children waved sparklers in the mild winter night – it was much less cold here than it had been in Mexico City. Cameron bought a bottle of tequila and he and Liam passed it back and forth between them. Both of them had been drunk before dinner was over, and were in a rhythm now that would carry on until neither of them could drink any more. If his parents knew how much they sometimes drank together, Liam thought, they would have reconsidered entrusting him to Cameron's care. He tilted the bottle again. The night flickered and spun. He threw his head back and stared at the sky. Above the floats he saw power cables strung between buildings in single strands, or gathered into sinewy tubes. They ran up and down walls like jungle vines.

They moved through the crowds as the procession

wound on, floats filled with drinkers and dancers, and paintings of the Virgin banded with flowers. The braid on the jackets and trousers of the mariachis caught the white of sparklers and yellow from the streetlights. Liam lost Cameron and stumbled alone down quieter streets, with no destination in mind. He decided to take every turn he came to. Some time later, he didn't know how long, he found himself in a blind alley where a sound system had been set up. The music, breakbeats and blaring trumpets, was deafening; it engulfed him. A man dancing beside him smiled and called out, but Liam couldn't hear what he said. Was it mockery, or was there desire in the way the man looked at him? He thought of Will in Soho Square. The man called out again, but turned away when Liam didn't answer. Liam drifted towards the wall of the alley and stared at the ragged posters for clubs and wrestling matches pasted across it. *Luz Roja*, one said, a red palm tree on white. *No cover*. He lit a cigarette and picked at the damp label of his beer: green and gold, with a picture of an Indian on it. Later, leaning against a wall somewhere, he watched pebbles on the ground move in diagonals, left to right, without ever getting anywhere. In his hand he held a white plastic bag containing a six-pack of beer and a bottle of mezcal.

He took a taxi back to the hotel. The brightly illuminated grounds were silent and empty. The bushes were emerald lumps, the trunks of the trees seared white by spotlights, the still swimming pool lit to a milky glow. Walking beside it, Liam thought of the Virgin, far to the south, standing on the seabed in the cold night water. He would write a letter, he thought, a letter that would tell Miguel everything. That would explain and change everything.

Cameron wasn't back from the fiesta. Liam opened the doors to the patio, turned on his bedside light and sat up on the bed, a pad of hotel notepaper resting on a book. He placed an ashtray on the pillow beside him. He alternated sips of mezcal with gulps of beer. *Time is always opposed to what is*, he wrote. Had he read that somewhere? He didn't know. He looked at it, crossed it out and took a new sheet of paper. Then he wrote it again. He wrote *M* above it, and the date. He didn't know where to begin. He and Miguel had never really talked about how they felt. In fact they had barely talked at all. He decided to write what he would say – what he thought he would say – if things were normal: if Miguel wasn't with Nuria, or maybe, he didn't know, if Miguel were a woman. Would that make any difference? He didn't think so. Once he started he had too much to say. He wrote fast and filled pages, the words bunching into jagged peaks and spreading into wormlike lines that spilled off the paper's edge and onto the cover of the book he was leaning on. He pressed down so hard that his writing veined the back of each sheet of paper. At some point, the sky pink through the open doors and birds calling, he reached for the mezcal bottle and found it was empty. The beer was all gone. Nothing seemed more terrible. He lifted the bottle and tossed it at the wall. The sound was incredibly loud, but as he stared at the shards, waiting, no one came to shout at him, or to ask him what was wrong. The silence hissed in his ears. He leafed through the letter: ten pages. He stretched and felt a wave of fatigue surge through his body.

When he woke up Cameron was standing above him. 'Li,' he said sorrowfully, 'you look like absolute fucking shit.' He shook his head and waved his hand around the room. 'What the fuck did you do in here?'

Liam lifted his head a few centimetres from the pillow and saw the stain on the wall where he threw the bottle, the broken glass beneath it.

'I'm going to breakfast,' Cameron said. 'See you whenever.' He slammed the door behind him: a spike driven through Liam's head.

When he got out of the shower the bathroom was clouded with steam, the mirror impenetrable. He didn't wipe it; he didn't want to see his face. Thinking about the day ahead made his stomach cramp. He put on a pair of black suit trousers and a white guayabera, an embroidered wedding shirt that had been provided for every male guest from overseas. Liam's seemed to be intended for a shorter, fatter man. Leaving the room he remembered the letter, which he found under his pillow. He started to read it, but stopped himself. He was afraid that if he read it he would throw it away, and then he would never know what could have happened. Passing reception on his way to breakfast he asked for an envelope, and stuffed the letter inside. With a shaking hand he wrote 'Miguel' on it. The letter felt heavy in his trouser pocket.

Cameron was sitting at a table beside the pool with two young women Liam recognised from Mexico City, cousins of Nuria. He waved Liam over, making a joke to the women about the sorry state of him. Liam wanted to ask Cameron where he had been all night, but it seemed too difficult to talk. Unable to eat breakfast, Liam shrugged at his ill-fitting shirt and drank cup after cup of black coffee. He knew it was ridiculous, but he felt like the cousins might know, just by looking at him, that he had fucked Miguel.

A few hours later, within the blessedly cool space of the church, he was shrugging still, slumped on the kind of hard, heavily varnished pew he remembered from the Sunday mornings of his childhood. He didn't pay much attention to the ceremony, but nevertheless found himself murmuring responses from memory. He felt himself tipping into sleep, and bit the inside of his mouth to wake himself up. He was incredibly thirsty, and a cut on his index finger – he had no idea where it was from – was throbbing painfully. Standing at one point, he watched a guest in the row in front of him – a German he had first met in Nice – run his hand down the back of his girlfriend's tight silk dress and tenderly squeeze first one half-grapefruit buttock, then the other.

There were four hundred guests, and outside the church lines of taxis and minibuses stretched down both sides of the street. The reception was at a finca outside town. Aperitifs were served on an island in the middle of a small lake, where two guitarists and a trumpeter moved through the crowd playing lulling music.

The more margaritas Liam drank, the better he felt. He stood at the bar drinking glass after glass. He chain-smoked. Every few minutes he stuck a finger into his back pocket to feel the letter.

For dinner they moved to a large, open-sided pavil-ion. On one side of it lay the lake, beyond which a steep wooded slope ran up to the finca. On the pavilion's op-posite side, a long grass lawn climbed gently to a dis-tant line of trees. 'When you get to your table, tip your waiter,' Nuria's elder brother had said. 'Your glass will never be empty.' Liam handed over all the money he had and drank several glasses of wine before the first course was served. He was sitting with two Mexican couples and a couple from Belgium he had spoken to in passing in Acapulco. When the Belgian woman asked him what he did he said, 'Nothing,' and when one of the Mexican men asked him how he knew Nuria and Miguel he said, 'I don't.' He was ignored after that. He looked around for Cameron but couldn't see him. Miguel and Nuria sat at a small table for two, in the centre of the floor, with a large belt of open space around them. Liam watched them eating, each one occasionally murmuring something that made the other smile. Miguel had his back to Liam, but Liam kept looking at him in the hope that he might turn around.

At the closest table to Miguel and Nuria sat the parents. Father talked to father, mother to mother. Liam decided the men were talking politics while the women spoke about Miguel and Nuria. Mothers always know their children better, he thought that was probably true. But they don't know everything. He tried to imagine Miguel's parents sharing a table with his own mum and dad. Even as a fantasy the image wouldn't cohere. All he could see were his parents sitting alone in some undefined space. How could he ever explain this to them?

As the starters were being cleared Liam raised his glass. 'Miguel and Nuria,' he said. Everyone at his table raised their glass and loudly repeated the toast. Hearing them, Miguel and Nuria looked over, smiled and raised their own glasses in response. The parents did the same, smiling curiously at Liam.

Liam made the same toast a few minutes later, as the main courses were being brought out. This time his tablemates didn't respond with the same enthusiasm, and the newlyweds didn't hear or acknowledge them. When Liam shouted their names again, a few moments later, he heard only uncertain laughter from those around the table. He sat in silence for a minute, then said, 'Miguel and Nuria,' quietly. He stood, knocking his cutlery noisily across his plate, and began to say something about the newlyweds being the sun and all the guests orbiting planets, but he lost his way. 'They are beautiful,' he said, which seemed like a way to end it, and fell backwards into his seat. He didn't say another word during dinner. When the waiter brought dessert, he left Liam a bottle of tequila.

As dinner ended a band started playing on a stage at one end of the pavilion. The tables were cleared and the dancefloor filled. Liam found himself on the stage with Cameron and a few other overseas guests. The bandleader was teaching them a complicated dance routine none of them could follow. A plank was brought out with five tequila glasses stuck in it, and they all had to squat and bend backwards at the same time to drink their shot. Later, Liam didn't know how much later, he was sitting with Cameron at the edge of the dancefloor, both leaning in so they could hear each other above the band. A half-empty bottle of tequila stood on the floor between them. 'What the fuck is wrong with you?' Cameron said. Liam felt like he was repeating the question, but didn't remember what they had been talking about. He wanted to find Miguel.

Cameron jabbed his shoulder. 'Are you listening to me?' he shouted.

Liam stood, shaking his head. 'I need to do something,' he said.

It was like stepping into a rowing boat, the way the ground lurched beneath him. He stumbled along the edge of the lake. He climbed the twisting path to the finca. The night air felt like a substance; it gathered itself in buzzing shapes. He walked under large, densely leaved trees and the darkness dripped down from the leaves and pooled at his feet. He stopped and stood still. Had he been going somewhere? He left the path and sat down at the base of a tree. He would give Miguel the letter and then he would stay. He would stay for as long as it took. He knew Miguel had feelings for him. It would be difficult, it would be painful, but it would be worth it. It was everything. He saw images of their life to come, like photographs. He stood up and wiped dirt from the seat of his trousers. He felt energy surge thickly inside him as he stretched his arms up towards the tree's black branches.

He strode back down to the pavilion, but when he reached it he couldn't go inside. He walked around it instead. It was quieter on the other side, and he leaned against a pole and looked in at the candlelit tables, at figures sitting and talking around them, and at the mass of bodies dancing just beyond. He saw Miguel leave the pavilion and walk off into the darkness. He followed. Miguel stopped, and Liam watched him light a cigarette. He wanted me to follow him, he thought, but when he said his name Miguel turned, startled. He started to speak but Liam cut him off. 'I'm going to stay in Mexico,' he said. As he spoke one hand went to his pocket and grasped the letter.

'You love México so much?' Miguel said.

'I love you.'

Miguel laughed. Liam shoved him. Miguel shoved him back. 'What are you even here for?' Miguel said.

'I came to see you,' Liam said. 'I came,' he hesitated, 'I came so we could be together.'

'This is my fucking wedding,' said Miguel. He poked a finger into Liam's chest. 'There's nothing between us. Nothing.'

Miguel's finger remained on Liam's chest. Liam gently closed his hand around Miguel's wrist. Miguel tore his hand away and then they were down, twisting on the grass. Liam pressed Miguel's face into the ground. Miguel put his knee in Liam's back. Liam put his arm across Miguel's throat and pressed down, then the world flipped and he was pinned, looking up, the stars crowding around Miguel's head. Miguel poked his finger in Liam's eye, a burning shock. He screamed and Miguel froze above him. Liam couldn't open his eyes. 'Lo siento,' he heard Miguel say, panting. Liam shrugged Miguel off and rolled over onto his knees, his eye jagged with pain. He heard Miguel move away, breathing loudly.

A few minutes later Liam re-entered the pavilion, hot and damp with sweat. He had grass stains on his shirt, which he saw was badly torn. Nuria was on the stage, singing with the band. Liam sat down at a table on the fringes of the pavilion, its empty chairs standing at angles to one another, and listened to her. Her voice was deep and strong. Two mariachis, dressed in baize green, accompanied her on guitar and trumpet. She scurried forwards and backwards, impelled by the drama of the song. She knelt down and cut the air with her hand. She pointed accusingly at the crowd, snapped her head away in disgust, then turned back to them with imploring eyes, the words coming from her like sobs.

Liam looked at the dirty glasses and crumpled napkins on the table. He snatched up a bottle of tequila, poured the dregs into a dirty glass and clapped loudly as the song finished. The pavilion lurched as if struck by a gust of wind. He looked at Nuria as she smiled and wiped tears from her eyes, giving small bows that were both joking and serious. Self-revulsion welled inside him. He pulled the letter from his pocket, took out his lighter and held it to one corner. The flame swelled around the paper. Liam rotated his wrist, the pages disappearing, until all that was left was the corner he held. He dropped it to the matted floor, let it burn a moment longer, then stamped it out.

Liam saw Miguel standing in a group, talking and smiling. He looked immaculate. Unsteadily Liam walked towards him, reached out and took his elbow. Miguel turned. He frowned, but tilted his head politely. 'I'm sorry about earlier,' Liam said, gesturing outside. 'I'm very sorry.'

Miguel took a moment to speak. 'There is nothing to apologise for,' he said. The people around Miguel looked at Liam curiously. Miguel smiled at them, inclined his head towards Liam and shrugged. They laughed at him as he swayed from side to side.

He tried to think of something else to say. 'I'm sorry,' he said, hearing the sloppiness of his speech. He turned away hopelessly. He concentrated on walking in a straight line as he shambled outside. Leaving the broad shore of light that spilled from the pavilion onto the grass, he stepped into the darkness. Shapes separated from the night as his eyes adjusted: trees and benches, clumps of drained glasses and bottles nestling in the grass. Behind him a chaos of music and voices. Ahead, empty space. He walked up the long grass slope that climbed away from the pavilion. The gradient was gentle but he was walking so fast that his calves quickly began to burn. He turned around and was surprised to see how distant the pavilion already was; he could have cupped it in his hand, or flattened it. Little sounds bled from its sides, chatter and dancing feet and drums knotted together, cut through by shrill cries and, sometimes, breaking glass. He could see some couples sitting on the grass just outside the pavilion, and waiters moving to and from the kitchen tent.

The world churned as he sat down heavily on the sloping ground. Tomorrow he would go back to London, to the book it was impossible to write and the TV and the silence. He lay flat and looked up at the stars. They spelled a message: burning fragments of his letter swept up from the lighter's flame and scattered across the black. The moon was a severed head. He knew he should go back to the wedding but he didn't want to move. He closed his eyes and passed in and out of sleep. He thought he heard Cameron and a woman's voice calling his name, but he ignored them. His phone rang and he pulled it out of his pocket and threw it away from him.

Later, he didn't know how much later, he saw a figure in white walking slowly up the slope. He hoped it was Miguel but knew it wasn't. He hoped it wasn't Nuria, knowing that it was. As she drew near he heard her dress rasping against the grass.

She stood over him. 'Here you are,' she said, sounding tired. 'The star of the show.'

'Sorry,' Liam said. 'I didn't mean to cause any trouble.'

'Oh-ho,' Nuria said, 'and how do you think you are doing?'

Liam tried to see the expression on Nuria's face, but she had her back to the distant lights of the pavilion. It was too dark to see.

'You have made me sad tonight, Liam.'

He wanted to stand but lacked the strength. 'I shouldn't have come,' he said.

'I love your brother, Liam. He is a special person for me. It was very important for him that you be here, but I think maybe it would have been better if you weren't.'

Realisation unfurled in Liam, like a flag catching the wind. 'You and Cameron.'

'A guest should behave better. Like Cameron, he knows how to behave.'

Liam wanted this to end. He worried about what she would say next. Still she stood before him, her dress glowing, her face dark.

'Do you think this is the way to repay your brother's kindness?' Her voice was low, calm.

Liam said nothing. Voices could be heard drifting up the hill, calling Nuria's name.

'I have watched you, Liam,' she continued, implacable. 'You think only of yourself.' She turned away. 'You will stay here?' she said over her shoulder. It sounded more like a command than a question.

Liam watched her walk down the slope, waving to the search party. He did not move. More time passed. The noise of music and voices became cars and voices, and dwindled to silence. He thought about walking back to Cuautla, about how far it was. He didn't know the way. He knew he could not see Miguel again. He needed to leave. Now. Tonight. But he could not move. He would obey Nuria. Insufficient as it was, it would be his apology. He lay flat on the grass and imagined he was hanging above the night. The trees pointed down into a gulf where the moon rolled like a ball and the stars wheeled, shooting light in spokes and spirals. The sky was a shattered pane of glass. He slept and woke and slept and woke to rabbits all around him, clinging to the grass with hunched intensity, their coats splashed silver. His eye ached. He heard a xylophone play – saw the light of his phone, dim in the distance – and fell back asleep. When he woke the air was crowded with birdsong, and he lay shivering in a net of dew. He saw red fingers slip around the edge of the sky. Dawn destroyed the stars.

THE CROSSING

Descending from Hawkridge, Ann and Jim came to the River Barle and what was marked on their map as a ford. The path ran to the water's edge and continued on the opposite bank some way downstream. The river wasn't more than thirty feet wide at this point, and the tea-coloured water didn't look deep, but it was impossible to go straight across and climb the opposite bank: a split-rail fence ran close to the water, with a barrier of alders and sedge crowded behind it. They needed to wade downstream to the continuation of the path. The river was moving rapidly, noisily sloshing over the jumbled rocks of its bed. Jim pointed out they were carrying everything they had brought with them for four days' hiking, and they didn't want to risk getting it soaked, did they? It was late September, and the first chill of autumn veined the air.

Ann was warmed now by a day's walking, but she remembered how frigid it had been when they left Dulverton early that morning. They woke before dawn, clutching each other tightly in the warm centre of the bed. The storage heater they fiddled with the previous evening had proved utterly ineffective: everything beyond their bodies lay frozen. They had only met a few weeks before, and Ann giggled nervously when she slipped out of bed and trotted, naked in the blue half-light, to the bathroom. She had lifted her feet exaggeratedly high and yelped at the floor's scathing coldness.

'We can go around,' she said, reading the map, 'but it's all the way back to that farmhouse.'

'Where those dogs were?'

She nodded.

'Miles back,' Jim said. He started taking off his boots. 'I'll go in without my pack first. See how slippery it is.' He stepped into the water, arms held out for balance. He sucked air through clenched teeth. 'Freezing,' he said.

Ann watched the river water wrinkle at his ankles, then his shins, then his knees. It darkened the folds of his trousers and pushed up to his thighs. He slipped, but recovered his balance.

'I'm all right, I'm all right,' he said hurriedly.

He sounded irritated, Ann thought. She watched him stop to survey.

'Looks like it gets deeper ahead,' he said, turning; then he reeled backwards. His arms thrashed and his hands grasped the air as he went over. His hand found a rock in the water and he froze in position, one side of his torso submerged.

'Oh!' Ann cried.

Still frozen in place, he looked back at her. His eyes were wide with surprise. His position made Ann think of a breakdancer mid-move, and she smiled.

'What's funny?' he said.

She laughed, thinking he wasn't serious. 'Your wounded pride.'

Back on the riverbank Jim took off his fleece and T-shirt and wrung them out. Ann watched as he jumped up and down to warm himself, admiring the bullish curve of his chest. 'I still think we can make it,' he said. 'Just need to be careful.'

She eyed the water dubiously. 'You said it gets deeper. I'll be in up to my waist at least.'

Rolling a cigarette, Jim shrugged agreement. He looked past her, back up the hill. 'Maybe the cavalry's arrived,' he said.

Ann turned and saw a man and a woman wearing matching red fleeces and black canvas trousers moving fast, their walking poles striking the ground with every step.

They were called John and Christine, and Ann guessed they were around fifty. They had the ruddy look of people who spent every weekend exposed to the elements. Jim explained about the map and the ford.

'Maps,' John said, with happy derision.

'We're not sure about it,' Ann said. 'Don't want our stuff getting drenched.' She felt this was too flimsy a reason for people like Christine and John, and was irritated that she had been the one to voice Jim's concern.

'What do you think?' Christine said to John.

'I'm not going back up that hill,' he said, grinning. 'No chance.'

'Well,' Christine said, looking between Ann and Jim, 'shall we all go together?'

'Yes!' Ann said with enthusiasm, masking the disappointment she felt that they wouldn't be crossing the river alone: it would be a lesser achievement now. She reached for Jim's arm. 'Will you be all right? Your pack's much heavier than mine.'

'Course I will,' said Jim, moving his arm away from her and adjusting the straps of his backpack, his eyes fixed on the ground. He jogged his pack up and down on his shoulders to straighten it.

They bagged their shoes and socks and rolled up their trouser legs. The mud of the riverbank was burningly cold against Ann's feet. Christine and John went in, ploughing through the water at speed. Jim stepped into the water carefully. When he was about halfway across Ann followed him, the first shock of the cold leaving her frozen in place.

The water's flow wasn't strong enough to tug, but some of the stones on the riverbed were sharp, and others slick with moss. Ann felt her feet slide a little beneath her. It was like walking on seaweed. She waited as Jim tested his footing. 'Bit tricky here,' he muttered over his shoulder.

'Move a little faster if you can, Jim,' she said. 'It'll be harder when your feet get numb.' She looked up at the grey sky. A bird call, a series of digital-sounding beeps, travelled over the water and received a reply from the opposite bank.

Up ahead, she saw Christine passing one of her poles back to Jim. John was on the far bank, fifteen feet downstream. 'You want this?' he called, holding a pole in the air.

'Yes please!' Ann said. John launched it into the air. To catch it she had to lean over so far that she almost fell. She yanked her body upright, willing herself to stay standing. Jim laughed; John and Christine clapped.

'Nice catch,' Jim said.

Pleased with herself, Ann pumped the air with the pole.

Now the crossing was simple. Beyond the river, in a field of close-cropped pasture, Ann and Jim took off their packs and sat on grass that seemed to radiate heat after the coldness of the water.

'Where are you guys headed?' Jim asked.

'Nepal,' John and Christine said, almost in unison. 'In a few weeks, that is,' John said. 'Just Winsford for now.'

'We're getting our walking legs into shape,' Christine said.

'Nepal, fantastic!' said Ann. She thought of how they had plunged into the water and saw them dropping, in matching outfits, into a crevasse.

The two couples set off in opposite directions. 'Make sure you take those poles with you,' Jim called after them, 'they're lifesavers.'

The walking that day had been all climbs and descents. It was a pleasure now to amble through flat pasture beside the chattering river. The clouds seemed to be thinning, and Ann felt warm after being immersed in the cold water. The strangled-sounding croaks of cock pheasants came from clumps of bilberry and heather edging the pasture. From time to time the birds' plump copper bodies could be seen scurrying from one patch of cover to another.

'Only a week till the shooting season starts,' Jim said.

'I didn't know you shot,' said Ann.

'I don't much,' Jim said.

'What do you shoot? Not animals, right?'

Jim paused and looked at her. 'No,' he said.

'Would you shoot an animal?'

He looked away. 'No,' he said.

He was lying. She knew he was lying. Several times, in the weeks since she met him, Ann had thought Jim was telling her what she wanted to hear. Even before she agreed to this weekend away the trait had been irritating her. Now she regretted having come. She had wanted to sleep with him as soon as she saw him, leaning against the kitchen counter at a party in a big, dilapidated house in Chalk Farm. And she had slept with him, but now she wished she had left it at that.

The sky continued to lighten. Wisps of cloud blew across a moon-white sun. A walking trip had been Jim's idea, and Ann had loved the thought of exploring a landscape, but she saw now that for him the pleasure lay in reaching a goal – twelve miles in a day, tick – while she was more interested in seeing things she might otherwise not. Earlier in the day, having established that Jim didn't know the names of most trees and flowers, she had tried to teach him some as they walked – hazel, alder, balsam – but it soon became clear he wasn't interested. Now she did it obstinately, pointing to a clump of clover-like leaves beside a kissing gate. 'Wood sorrel,' she said.

Jim barely looked where she had pointed. He pushed the gate open for her. Earlier in the day they had made an event of these gates, puckering their lips exaggeratedly. On a quiet woodland path just before the climb up to Hawkridge, their kiss had developed into something more serious as they passed through the gate – she was here anyway, she thought, and he was sexy even if he was annoying. Ann had backed against a tree, tugging Jim after her. She was gripping his erection through his trousers when she heard the clinking of camping gear, and they were still arranging themselves when a pair of older, silver-haired walkers strode past, packs swaying. Breezily they said hello, then fell laughing against each other after the strangers had passed. Now, angry at the lie, Ann still lifted her face as they passed through the gate but kept her mouth closed against the thrust of Jim's tongue. She made a joke of it. 'Wait till we're in Withypool,' she said, swatting his chest.

'Ah, Withypool,' Jim said with mock awe, 'the Paris of Somerset.'

They continued moving upriver. The rushing water flashed blackly beside them. Jim was looking at something as they passed, and Ann turned to see a short metal ladder and a small cage affixed to the side of an oak.

'For hunting?' she said.

'Guess so,' he said.

Ann shook her head. Looking away, towards the water, she saw an uneven path of stepping stones running across the river. They stood from its surface like the vertebrae of a giant animal. 'Look!' she said. She reached into the thigh pocket of Jim's combat trousers for the map. She spread the map on the ground and traced her finger across it. Withypool lay on the other side of a steep ridge. 'If we cut across,' she said, 'we'll avoid the climb completely.'

Jim crouched down beside the river, his back to Ann.

'Jim, what d'you think? It knocks about a mile off. We could be in Withypool in less than half an hour.'

He still didn't answer. Ann stood and walked over to him. The river was deeper here, and running fast. The large, irregularly shaped stones standing proud of the water were a mottled grey, their corners furred with dark green moss. The ones that sat lower in the flow were black and glossy like a killer whale's skin.

An arrow of sun pierced the cloud and struck the running water, sending sparks skidding over its surface. It turned the foam fringing the stones gold, and for a moment the water became too brilliant to look at. It roared like a crowd in Ann's ears. Jim stood.

'Well?' Ann said, shrugging. 'Man or mouse?'

Jim smiled at her and looked away. 'Nah,' he said. 'Let's stick to the plan.'

'Really?' said Ann. She kept her voice light, but disappointment yawned in her. 'Could be fun?' she said.

'Yeah.' Jim sounded unconvinced. 'I think we had our fun for the day back there. It looks easy, I know, but the water's deeper here. One slip and it's goodbye dry gear. Tomorrow'd be a joke in wet clothes.' He picked up the map and folded it away as he started walking, then turned around and took a few steps backwards. 'Come on,' he said, 'Guinness on me when we get there.'

Ann forced a smile and gave him a thumbs up. She

looked from one stepping stone to the next, to a cluster of white flowers nodding just above the water on the far bank. Seventeen stones. She threw a handful of plucked grass into the current and watched as the blades were snatched rapidly away.

Jim was already a good distance ahead, ascending the ridge; above him a group of sheep moved away at his approach. Keep going, you arsehole, Ann thought. She climbed after him. She wanted to be on her own, but didn't know how Jim would react if she crossed the river without him. She couldn't be bothered dealing with his anger, or worse, his sulking. At the top of the field, she turned just as the sun broke out again. The river ran white with light. She saw herself halfway across it, jumping from stone to stone towards the bright, empty fields beyond.

The path climbed into a wood. Ann stepped up old stone steps with risers more than a foot tall. Rivulets streaked the steep hillside. Some of them held no more than a trickle, while in others the water gushed down to join the river that now lay far below. Ann couldn't see Jim, but she could smell his acrid tobacco smoke. She swatted the air and rubbed her eyes. She felt tired, and angry with herself for being here at all. Why did she always prolong things when she knew they weren't going to work? She fought an urge to stop walking and lie down beside the path. She passed another field of sheep, their coats marked with sprays of blue dye. Most of them were shambling away from the fence: Jim's living wake. Only one sheep stood its ground, a black-faced animal that held Ann's gaze as she passed, its jaw working on a hank of grass. 'Good afternoon, Mr Sheep,' she called, saluting the way her mum had taught her to greet magpies. The sheep blinked, and its tail flickered from side to side as it pushed a sequence of turds onto the ground behind it.

Ann found Jim further uphill, idly whacking a bush with a stick. The climb became a descent, and before long they stepped off the earth track onto the tarmac of the Withypool road. Ferns covered the high banks on either side, and branches of oak and beech joined to form a tunnel. Soon they were passing stone cottages and barns, the only signs of life the threads of smoke rising from chimneys.

They had booked a room at the Willow Tree, whose custard-yellow walls and blue windows reminded Ann of a witch's gingerbread house. She eased herself gratefully onto the bench of a trestle table that stood on a flagstone terrace above the road. The only other people drinking outdoors were a man and woman with a pair of velvet-brown pointers lying at their feet. The dogs stayed down, but their eyes rebounded from Jim to Ann to their owners. The owners nodded hello, and continued their conversation in low voices.

'Drink?' Jim said.

'Oh god yes,' said Ann, smiling. 'Guinness. Pint please.' Jim went inside the pub. Ann took off her boots and stretched her legs. They had walked more than ten miles of hilly ground that day, and now she was sitting down she felt like she might never stand up. Her legs were packed with wet sand. The dogs regarded her, their sides swelling and shrinking in unison. Looking up from them, she found the man staring at her. The woman, her back to Ann, was hunting through her bag for something. The man took a sip from his pint, his eyes never leaving Ann's. She knew what that look wanted. He was rangy, strong-looking in brown Barbour and muddy jeans. His sharp jaw was mossed with a couple of days' growth of beard, his eyes were dark, unblinking. Then the woman produced a lighter from her bag, and the man turned towards her and pushed a pack of cigarettes across the table.

Jim returned with two black pints. The stout was cold and thick and Ann drank deeply, the beer's creamy head forming a moustache that spread from her nostrils to her cheeks. Jim laughed, then tipped his glass so far back that he coated his nose, and rivulets brown as river water streaked across his cheeks to his ears. Now Ann laughed. The dog owners looked on in silence. Screw yourselves, Ann thought, thinking she might as well enjoy herself even as it all collapsed. She raised her pint in another toast. They clashed glasses and gulped down the cold, black beer.

#

From the window of their low-ceilinged room at the top of the inn Ann saw the purple and brown heights of Exmoor rising in the distance, beyond ranks of beech, oak and birch. She was wearing a towel and kneeling on the worn cushions of a bench seat. The bedside lamps threw out a bronze light. From the bathroom came the sound of running water.

Jim leaned out of the bathroom door, eyebrows arched. 'I think we can both fit in that tub, you know.'

'Sounds good to me,' Ann said. 'You get in, I'll be there in a second.'

She heard a gasp of pleasure and pain as Jim eased himself into the hot water. Ann fetched her phone to take a picture of the twilight view. The grey sky and green trees – not a trace of autumn visible yet – blended in a vividness she knew a photograph wouldn't capture, but she tried anyway. She viewed the image: useless. Better just to look at it, she thought.

Jim called her name. He was lying back in the bath. She motioned for him to lean forward and she took off her towel, placed it on the tiled shelf at the end of the bath and sat on it. She held Jim's shoulders and moved him back so that he lay between her knees. His body was broad, and she needed to widely splay her legs to make room for him. She felt the surface of the hot water as a tightness around her shins. She leaned down, scooped up some water and poured it slowly over Jim's scalp. Slicked to his skull, his hair glistened like wet stone.

The day was ending and the bathroom, lit only by a skylight, was dim. In the near-dark Ann leaned Jim's body forward and washed his back. His pale skin shone faintly in the darkness. He murmured her name, his face close to the water. He reached an arm forward and turned the tap, adding hot water to the cooling bath. Ann's hands, coated in soap foam, worked their way from his neck down to his kidneys. She ran the sides of her thumbs up over the ridges of his spine. She noticed a chain of moles, flush with his skin, running along his shoulder blades. She put her hands in the water and cleared his back of soap. He started to lean back but she pushed him forward again. He rested his face on his knees. He said something she couldn't make out. She put her finger on the leftmost mole and walked her hand across them, left to right and right to left. 'You're marked,' she said. She waited for a reply, but all she heard was the deep, oblivious breath of a man asleep.

#

'Do you think we'd have made it across?' Ann asked at dinner in the pub dining room.

'Across what?' Jim said, around a mouthful of steak.

'The stepping stones.'

'Oh. Yeah. Sure. Why?'

'I don't know. You seemed . . . scared?'

'Scared?' Jim's cutlery clattered against his plate. A couple at the table beside them turned at the sound. 'Are you serious? Course I wasn't scared. A bit cautious, maybe, that's all.'

'My mistake.'

'Listen,' Jim said, straightening in his seat, 'wet gear is no joke—'

Ann started to smile.

'What's funny?' he said.

She only shrugged, as if to say it wasn't important.

After dinner she suggested a walk, but Jim said he was tired and they had an early start in the morning. 'Bit too dark and scary out there for me, anyway,' he added, which she had to give him credit for. She thought about going out on her own, but found she was too tired, after all. Back in the room they undressed, put on robes that had been left out for them, and lay on the bed watching TV. Ann felt restless. She was bored by what they were watching, and rolled on her back to stare at the beams in the ceiling, listening to the film Jim was so absorbed in. It was about a series of bank robberies, each more elaborate and violent than the last. When it ended Jim said he was going to sleep. Ann asked if he minded her light being on. 'No,' he said, but instead of turning away put his arms around her and gathered her towards him. She opened her mouth to his kiss. One last time, she thought. Why not? His hand moved inside her robe. His thumb began circling the nipple. She drew him down on top of her. She closed her eyes and saw him striding away from her up the ridge, away from the river. He entered her and she felt a lump at her throat that she let out in a low moan. The river ran fast past the stepping stones, another world away. He pulled out of her, his quick breath hot against her cheek. She gripped him and squeezed, feeling the semen surge across her belly. He rolled off her and reached down with his hand and fumbled at her until she pushed his hand away. 'Sleep,' she said. He murmured something and again moved his hand towards her, but she pushed it back again. She reached up and switched off the light. She lay in the dark listening to the sound – so faint – of purling water. She started to touch herself and pushed herself back against the mattress. She was crossing the room, opening the door. The stairs creaked. The boot room was cold. She climbed away from the village, up past the rivulets' trickle and wash, past silent trees and sleeping sheep, and emerged at the top of the ridge above the river. Moonlight frosted the fields and scorched the water silver. Descending, the water's noise grew. The moon lay on the river in a serrated white line, stretching and gathering with the water's movement.

The stones were a chain of black squares in the liquid silver. Across the water rose the mass of the moor. On the far bank he stood, in his Barbour and jeans. She crossed the stones, flecks of icy water against her shins. He crossed, and they met in the river's flow. He pushed her down and was inside her. She straddled him and worked herself up and down the length of him. She pressed her palms against the cold, wet rock. As she came she leaned down into the fast-running brightness of the water, plunging her face into its icy grip.

#

When Ann woke her irritation with Jim had swollen into anger. They ate breakfast in near silence, and exchanged few words as they walked. She had decided that when they reached that day's goal she would tell Jim she was going back to London. All she wanted was to be away from him.

The day was cloudy and cool: good for walking. They decided to avoid roads, so their route bypassed the village of Exford and took them towards a smaller crossing over the Exe. About half a mile before that, however, they came to a fast, narrow stream just ten feet across that wasn't marked on the map. The banks on both sides were very steep: the grey water, crested in places with curds of white foam, hissed past a good six feet below them. A split tree trunk had been laid between the banks, long ago judging by how embedded in the path it was.

Ann saw Jim hesitate, looking downstream and then up. 'I'm sure there's a long way round,' she said. 'Better safe than sorry, right?'

Jim turned and started to say something, then turned away. He walked onto the log bridge and was halfway across – Ann had just placed a foot on the splintered wood – when he lost his balance, crouched, yanked himself back upright for a moment, then flipped backwards and down into the water. He was carried under the bridge and Ann saw his head strike a group of jagged stones. He lay face down in the water. Carried swiftly, he was snatched round a bend and was gone, and it was that Ann never forgot: the terrible speed of it.

THE COLOSSUS OF RHODES

My family has come to Cephalonia. My daughters, four
and two, have never had a beach holiday before. Mostly we go to Sweden to visit my wife's family. This year,
though, is different. This year my wife said: 'Sun. A guar-
anteed week of it.' And so here we are, lying on sun loungers and running into the water and out of the water, and
turning brown by degrees.

It's my first time back in Greece since I was ten, when
my family went to Rhodes. I remember spending nearly
all my holiday money on a game called Crossbows and
Catapults. I was always playing games, mostly ones with
knights and spells and monsters. In this one you had to
destroy your opponent's castle with plastic pellets fired
by your catapult and your crossbow, the giant kind of
crossbow that I knew was called a ballista, because back
then I was really up on my medieval military hardware.

The box seduced me. It had a picture of a battle on
it. A bearded Greek was turning and shouting, as if you,
the game's owner, were rushing into the fray right behind
him. Up ahead, a large blue disc was about to strike a

group of cowering soldiers. The Greek's opponents, barbarians, had flung the disc from a catapult positioned in
the distance, beyond a red river. They were the standard
kind of barbarian: leather jerkin, fur loincloth, horned
helmet; everything they wore had once been alive. Behind
them their fortifications lay in ruins. The Greeks had fired
their own catapult, too, and the foremost barbarian's
arms were raised towards the speeding red disc. He wel-
comed death with a yell, spittle falling from his mouth in
strings. Like I said, the standard kind.

The rest of my money went, as I remember it the same
day, on a pair of 'Punky' sunglasses, a cheap curve of
black plastic with mirrored lenses that instantly became,
alongside a white Lacoste sweatband inherited from a
cousin, my favourite article of clothing. All I wanted to
do was wear my sunglasses and go back to our hotel to
play my new game. I didn't care that I'd be playing alone:
my brothers, five and seven years older than me, liked
football and snooker, not swords and magic and made-up
stuff.

#

On the second day my mum, my brothers and I got stuck
in the small hotel lift. We were only a couple of feet above
the third floor and tried forcing the doors, but we couldn't

get them more than a few inches apart. 'Help!' we called, but no one answered.

'Don't worry,' my mum said, 'your dad will work out where we are.' Frank and Dominic were excited, making jokes about running out of air and saying they'd climb out through the roof: they knew how, they said, because they'd seen it in a film. The lift was hot. I stared at a strand of my mum's red hair that was stuck in a curl on her forehead. I thought about there being nothing below us but empty space, and how the wire we were hanging from might fray and snap. I concentrated on not crying. My brothers would call me a baby if I cried.

My mum had found her phrasebook. 'Vo-e-*thee*-ah,' she said. 'That's "help" in Greek. Vo-e-*thee*-ah.'

'Vo-e-*thee*-ah,' we repeated uncertainly.

'That's right, very good,' she said. She spoke the word more loudly. She pitched her voice very high and sort of sang it, in the voice she used to call our cat. 'Vo-e-*thee*-ah,' she said. 'Vo-e-*thee*-ah.'

Just when I felt sure we would be left to hang there forever, voices came back, faint but distinct. Mum smiled at me and puffed some air up out of her mouth in relief, freeing the stuck curl. She called out loudly, 'Vo-e-*thee*-ah!'

We all joined in and the lift rang with the word: 'Vo-e-*thee*-ah!'

The voices answered again, this time from just beyond the lift doors. 'No,' one of them said kindly, 'no. Vo-*ee*-thee-ah.'

#

My wife wanted sun, but it terrifies her. We spend what seems like hours each day coating our daughters in sunblock, until their limbs slip from our grasp. Then we coat ourselves. The youngest, Nora, thinks sunblock looks, smells and tastes delicious, and I'm constantly batting her arm out of her mouth. 'More cream,' she says, eyeing the bottle thirstily. I worry that one day I'll find her guzzling it.

#

I ignored the rules that came with Crossbows and Catapults in favour of my own, something I did a lot back then. In the regular game the figures of the Greeks and barbarians were little more than set dressing, but in my version they became much more important. I recycled some basic combat rules that used six-sided dice rolls to determine who won each round, and how much damage they inflicted. I kept a record of hit points on a pad, and when a piece was killed it wasn't removed from play but lay dead on the battlefield. This was important. The record of the carnage was my favourite part of the game: the pattern of corpses told the story of the battle. Studying it between turns flooded me with excitement, like the moment in hide-and-seek when the seeker shouts comingreadyornot and a fizz of anticipation crawls through your body, from between your legs right up to your scalp.

When I was playing it was like it was real: the war machines, the fallen walls and the heaped bodies all transformed from plastic into wood, stone and flesh. I moved around the field of battle and pressed my head against the ground to see it up close. I can remember the feel of the cool tiles of the hotel-room floor against my cheek. Sometimes I stayed in one position for so long my breath made a pool of condensation on the tile, as smoke drifted and moans carried on the wind.

#

When she's with her sister, most of the games devised by my eldest, Sonja, revolve around exclusion and repeated demonstrations of the arbitrary. The exact amount of time it takes can vary, but one moment the girls will be playing well together, fussing over the care and comfort of a group of dolls, or driving plastic cars around an imaginary network of streets, and then, having turned my back for less than a minute to send an email or fetch something from another room, I look up and Nora is in tears, surrounded by a great emptiness, while Sonja is happily playing with all the toys in another corner of the room. Or else whatever game they were playing has metamorphosed into a prison scenario, Nora invariably the prisoner as Sonja stalks up and down outside her cell, cackling like a sadist.

When I see it I'm glad my brothers were so much older, and mostly left me alone.

#

My parents rented a car to explore the island and we travelled south from Rhodes Town, towards Lindos. There was no air conditioning so we drove with all the windows open, and the car filled with rushing wind that snatched at the pages of my *Fighting Fantasy* book. Mum told me to stop reading and pay attention to where we were, so I looked out of the window for the shortest amount of time I could get away with. I saw low green hills covered in bushes, and trees with pink and purple flowers.

'Myrtle and thyme,' Mum shouted over the wind, pointing out of the window. I saw birds that looked like pigeons flying between the short trees. To the left, past a drowsing Dominic, was a sea so still it could have been a painted blue floor. The world was fine, but it wasn't much beside a book.

We drove to a place called St Paul's Bay, the beach empty despite the heat. The bay was almost sealed off from the water by two arms of rock. On one side the rock was low and looked like the head of a duck lying flat against the water. On the other, stretching much further into the sea, ran a series of cliffs that might have been a vast slumbering dragon. Flecks in the rock made the cliffs glint as if they were scattered with tiny mirrors. We set up camp under a solitary pine tree, where the sand was less gravelly. White butterflies, like scraps of paper, flapped around us.

Thinking of the previous day's battle, I saw Greeks and barbarians positioned on either side of the bay hurling missiles across the water. The Greeks were winning, but the barbarians yelled and cheered and shook their weapons just the same. One of them bent and bared his bottom, laughing as he slapped his cheeks.

Mum wanted to go for a swim, and because no one else wanted to go with her I said I would. Dominic, Frank and Dad, in T-shirts and shorts, lay on towels in the sun. The sun glared off their white skin so much that it hurt to look.

We edged into the cold water and stood beside each other. Mum had coated me in sun cream, and I stood watching the water around my knees go oily. 'St Paul was shipwrecked here,' she said, standing with her hands on her hips. 'That's why it's called St Paul's Bay. You know who St Paul is, don't you?'

'They read his letters out at Mass.'

'That's right.'

We waded further into the water, which began to feel warmer. It was clear, with a light green tinge. The pale sand shifted under our feet. Tiny ribbons of seaweed hung in the water.

'Paul persecuted the followers of Jesus when he was a young man,' Mum said, 'but when he was travelling to Damascus, Jesus appeared to him.'

If I had read about this in a fantasy novel I would have been rapt, but everything with the taint of church had all the wonder drained out of it. It was the longest hour of each week. As Mum spoke my attention drifted, and I looked towards a small white chapel at the edge of the bay. An old man was locking the door with a padlock. He walked to the edge of the water, his hands in his pockets, and spat a long brown stream onto the rocks below.

'. . . and that's why,' Mum said as we leaned forward into the water and began to breaststroke, our fingertips just touching, 'he began travelling around . . . the Mediterranean . . . preaching,' squeezing her words between breaths as we swam faster. I soon wanted to turn around. I wasn't used to swimming in the sea, and although the water was quite shallow I didn't like – still don't like – the thought of space below me in which something might be moving. My imagination fills the void.

'And he actually came here?' I asked, to distract myself from this predicament as much as anything. I stopped swimming and began to tread water.

'That's right,' Mum said, stopping a little further ahead, 'he sailed into a storm and he was shipwrecked, right here in this bay.'

I saw bearded men dragging each other from the foaming water, their soaked robes sleek as otter pelts. Rain fell from a dark sky. Fragments of wood and shreds of sail churned in the water. I felt a tentacle snake around my feet and thrashed my legs to get away, but it was only a current of colder water. Towards the shore I saw a golden rock rising from the sea and I longed to be sitting on it. To be touched only by air. I swam towards it, my breathing shallow with growing panic. When I reached the rock I scrambled onto it. The water running off me turned the gold stone grey.

#

Because Anna and I don't drive we're reliant on taxis and buses, which on Cephalonia isn't ideal. Luckily, for some unfathomable reason, our eldest daughter loves waiting for the bus. She thinks it's sophisticated. She stands apart from us and looks around in a way she considers extremely grown-up: mouth puckered with dissatisfaction, nose imperiously raised. 'I'm waiting for the bus,' she says haughtily to whomever happens to be closest to her. Since she was born I've tried to maintain a record of this kind of thing – attitudes, mispronunciations, nonsense stories she tells – and when I go back to it I'm amazed by how much I've already forgotten.

#

I remember a morning spent wandering around Mandráki Harbour. Standing on the harbour wall, Dad pointed out some brown smudges above the blue horizon. 'Turkey,' he said.

The harbour was where the Colossus of Rhodes had once stood: one of the Seven Wonders of the World. The guidebook said it couldn't have really stood astride the harbour the way so many paintings show; its weight would have been too great. But everywhere we went I saw postcards of it with one foot on each wall, and anyone walking out to the mouth of the harbour couldn't help but stare across from one stone pier to the other and think, 'This is where it was.' I stood there and saw it rising a hundred feet above me, the same emerald green as the Jolly Green Giant, naked except for a loincloth. It faced the sea, a bow and quiver on its back and one arm raised and holding a burning torch. I imagined myself aboard a merchant ship sailing between the Colossus's legs. We sailors craned our heads as the sun disappeared and we entered into the lake of shadow beneath the vast statue. The noise of the busy harbour, the slap of waves against the boat's hull and the cries of birds overlapped and echoed. A chill haze of salt spray hung in the air.

I imagined the sloping foot of the Colossus beside me on the harbour wall, its toenails big as turtle shells. It collapsed in an earthquake, the story goes, and lay rusting for hundreds of years, and when it was sold for scrap it took a thousand camels to take it all away.

#

I remember a couple of other things. Not other things: the main thing. I was in a cafe playing an arcade game. My brothers, I think, had gone back to the hotel. Mum and Dad, I think, were in a neighbouring shop buying crockery. They bought me a Coke and gave me a stack of coins for the game. I'm not sure that's how it was, and it seems strange that I would have been left alone, but I had to have been alone, or at least distant enough from everyone that I felt alone, and the game I was playing was definitely Asteroids, which I do remember because it was a game I never liked; I always struggled to correct for the inertia that dragged my ship where I didn't want to go.

I was sitting on a barstool, my Coke on a table behind me. The arcade game was beside the window, through which I saw a car park and beyond it the smooth water of the harbour. The bright sun made it difficult to see the screen. The heat made my thighs stick to the leather seat, and a crack in the cushion pinched my skin as I squirmed in unison with the chaotic movements of my ship.

A man came and stood close beside me. Right away it felt strange, the closeness. He said something I didn't understand and I turned to look up at him. He had a kind face, pudgy and tanned. His hair was black and lay in curls at his collar. He smiled down at me, and I smiled back. My palms prickled. I crashed into another asteroid. I looked down at the man's loose trousers, his sandals, his feet. There were spots of white paint on his toes. He spoke again and put his hand on my leg, just above the knee. I looked at the screen and saw my ship spinning, spinning. I looked around and saw the owner of the place standing behind the counter reading a newspaper. A woman sat at a table, staring at her plate as she chewed her food. Voices gabbled from a radio. The man lifted his hand and placed it halfway up my thigh. He murmured something that sounded like encouragement and gestured at the screen with his free hand while the other kneaded my thigh. He had a friendly smile. I continued to smile, not knowing what else to do. When I looked back at the screen several asteroids were closing in. My hands were frozen. My ship shattered into three lines that floated apart and slowly faded into the black. The man's hand, heavy on my thigh, moved slightly, and he exhaled through his nose. I felt that warm expelled air run across my cheek and down my neck. I felt his fingers flex, and one of them came to rest against the tip of my penis. GAME OVER, the screen said. I spun the ball as his finger began to roll backwards and forwards, backwards and forwards.

I pressed my hands against the game cabinet, kicked back my stool and ran to the door. It was locked, and as I pushed helplessly against it I could hear the other people in the cafe moving quickly towards me. The air grew thicker, hotter. I yanked and the door opened: I had pushed when I needed to pull. I turned and saw the man still standing beside the arcade machine; the woman still staring at her plate; at the counter the owner looked up from his paper and towards me at the door with weary curiosity. 'Goodbye!' I shouted at all of them, and ran outside.

That night my family went for a walk after dinner, but I didn't want to go. I asked to go back to the room instead. I said I was tired. Mum went up to the room with me, and told me to lock the door and not open it to anyone. 'I'll be back in an hour,' she said. After she had gone I got my game from the cupboard, opened the box and took out the pieces.

#

Nora has sunburn. It's my fault. We fell asleep together on a sun lounger and the sun swung around and now her foot has a stripe, red as a ribbon, running across the heel. She cried and cried, and couldn't sleep at all the night after it happened. For a while, silently and ridiculously, I blamed my wife for wanting this holiday in the sun. Now we make a thing of moisturising the burn. 'Foot drinking,' my daughter says, watching carefully as I rub in, as gently as possible, the chill white liquid. 'It's so cold!' Nora says, looking at me, her eyes widened in a rehearsed and pleasurable surprise. She wears her socks on the beach, only taking them off when she goes into the sea. When we are back in London her skin will peel, revealing the next layer, and before long she – we – won't even remember the pain she suffered.

#

Ippotón Street, the Street of the Knights, ran down towards the harbour between buildings of biscuit-coloured stone. In the late afternoon a diagonal stripe of shadow divided the street. I pretended the sun was lethal: stepping outside the shadow meant death. The street was busy with tourists leaving the Old Town and heading to the harbour for sunset.

Absorbed in my game, I didn't realise how far I had dropped behind my family. Halfway down the street, almost hidden in the shadow of an alcove, I saw a cat curled into a circle. As I approached it lifted its head, its eyes open to slits, and let out a quavering miaow. It was very thin, and its black-and-white fur was matted with dirt. Crouching down beside it I saw a deep wound on its neck. It had a thick, pale yellow goo around its eyes. It was obviously dying. Tentatively I reached out to stroke its back. Its fur was sticky with dirt. Very slowly, as if immensely tired, it moved its head back over its shoulder, feebly seeking my hand. I stood and looked around. Crowds of people were passing, but no one was paying any attention to me. I scuffed my leg backwards and forwards a couple of times. The sole of my trainer whispered against the smooth stone of the pavement. I swung my leg again, harder, and felt the faintest resistance as my foot brushed against the cat's head; it made another small pleading sound. I can help, I thought. I swung my leg again, then rested my palms against the wall and shut my eyes and kicked as hard as I could. I heard a crunch, like a Coke can being flattened. I opened my eyes to look, then turned to face the street. The crowds walked on, oblivious.

#

On the last day before going home we went back to St Paul's Bay. It was overcast, the tide was out, and in the grey light the golden rock looked more like a lump of cement dumped in the dull water. I kicked pinecones across the sand and thought about what I'd do for the rest of the summer.

Dad walked out from behind a bush in his trunks. 'Sure you don't want to swim?' he said.

I shook my head. I sat down on the sand and listened to cries of pain carrying over the water. At the mouth of the bay, missiles flitted back and forth. The Greeks had the higher ground and the barbarians were being slaughtered. The sea, stained red, was nearly solid with the corpses of men and animals. In the sky a spacecraft spun wildly. Beside the church at the side of the bay the old caretaker was scrubbing a stained patch of wall.

The battle went on and on. My family ignored it. They swam in the bloody water as the Greeks' missiles climbed slowly into the sky and sped downwards. The barbarians threw up their arms and bellowed to meet them, brave and full of hate.

#

My family went on holiday to Rhodes in 1985, more than thirty years ago. There were many times when I thought about telling my parents what happened, but I never did. The more time that passed, the less certain I became that I should tell them. And now I've written this it already seems more real than whatever 'actually' happened, even though there's so much I left out. Like Kostas, our waiter at Top 13, the restaurant we went to, as I remember it, every single night of the holiday. My middle brother, a gifted caricaturist, drew a picture of Kostas and gave it to him as a present. In the picture he was lifting his arms heroically, carrying three huge trays loaded with food while bikini-clad women clung to his legs. He gave us his pen, a cheap plastic biro with the name of the restaurant printed on it in golden block capitals. It was a prized possession at first, one my brothers and I fought over, but sooner or later it lost its allure and became just another pen in a pot.

We met an American woman called Nancy on an excursion to a ruined temple or a ruined fort; I forget which. She was a teacher, and was living in London for a year on an exchange programme. We stayed in touch, and five years later the whole family travelled to Corvallis, Oregon to visit her. A few years after that, when I was travelling around the US, her daughter Karla put me up in New York.

But there isn't any room for them here. Stories need everything extraneous to be stripped away, and Nancy and Kostas, let alone Karla, are extraneous. So are my brothers, who are barely present at all. I probably should have left them out altogether, but I couldn't bring myself to. Plus, my being an only child would have raised other questions, like 'Why did his parents leave him alone in the cafe?'

Which is a good question anyway. I can't remember where they were when I encountered that man. I find it hard to believe they weren't there – around a corner maybe; I remember the arcade game being in a sequestered space, the kind of side room where you might find a pool table tucked away, or air hockey. When I tried writing it like that, though, with them so close by, it seemed implausible. Other than that, what I describe is faithful to my memory of the event. It would have been more dramatic if the guy had started masturbating himself like the tramp in the Joyce story, but he didn't.

What I didn't do is kill a cat. But I did see a cat get killed. It really was on Ippotón Street, and I might well have been playing that game with the sun, I used to do stuff like that all the time. I saw this kitten curled against the wall (it's a cat in the story because a kitten would be too much). It was dirty and sick, and as I was stroking it a group of Greek kids surrounded me. The leader, a boy maybe a year or two older than me, started shouting. I didn't understand what he was saying, but he was obviously angry. He pushed me down on the ground and kicked the kitten two or three times until it was dead. Cats are pests there.

And I shut my penis in my zip. Another thing I never told my family. We were going to dinner, Dad and my brothers were already downstairs in the lobby, and Mum was waiting for me just outside the toilet door. She wasn't hurrying me, but I felt like I was keeping everyone waiting. I shook off and quickly yanked up the zip of my trousers. Too quickly. I won't try and describe the pain. It's enough to say I looked down and saw these angry pink bubbles of flesh squeezed between the zip's teeth. I tried writing about stifling my tears, about wadding toilet paper into my pants, about the scar I was left with, but I scrapped it. Boy gets felt up, sees kitten being kicked to death, then rips penis up in zip? What's anyone meant to do with a story like that?

The funny thing is, the scar on my penis (a line of raised, caramel-coloured skin as thin as a credit card) is the only tangible evidence I have of anything that happened in Rhodes. The sunglasses broke and were thrown away, I lost the sweatband, and Crossbows and Catapults was exiled to a cupboard shelf before being donated to a jumble sale along with boxes of other once-prized possessions.

Maybe it's because I never spoke about these things to anyone that I find it so difficult to shape them into a story now. And if I can't do that, what are the chances anyone else will? When, if, my parents and brothers hear about the man, or the cat, or my penis, it will only confuse them. 'Are you sure it really happened that way?' they'll say. 'Can it have been like that?' It's understandable. It was thirty years ago, and even if what I've described were objectively true, what does it mean if no one else knows about it? And what will change if people do know? What difference does writing about it make? Maybe it's easier to say I made it all up.

But when I look at my daughters squatting on the sand, burying their toys and making little streets and houses with shells, I can't help but wonder: if the same thing happened to them, would I want to know? And if I knew, what then? Would I find the man who did it? Report him? Beat him? Kill him?

I've rarely spoken to anyone about what happened on Rhodes, but not so long ago, when I started thinking about this story, I described it to a lawyer I met at a party and she laughed and said, 'And that happened to you once? That happens to girls hundreds of times. After a while it's not even news.'

Can that really be true? I tell myself it can't, of course it can't. Saying something doesn't make it true, nor does silence strip the truth of its authority. I know what happened to me, and that I won't let it happen to these girls I can still enfold in my arms, and who jiggle their feet on my thighs. It's impossible to say they will always be safe, but sometimes it can feel like the truth, the same way that when you stand at the mouth of Mandráki Harbour you can see the Colossus soaring above you. I tell the girls about the statue that was the biggest the earth had seen, that took twelve years to build, and that one day fell and a thousand camels came to take it all away. 'Is it true, Dad?' Sonja asks. 'Did it really happen like that?' And I say of course it's true, every word.

INNSBRUCK

Many swear that the loveliest village on the Costa Brava is Cadaqués – a cluster of brilliant white buildings surrounded by olive groves, hugging a turquoise bay dotted with colourful fishing boats. Both it and the surrounding area blend wind, water, light and rock to enchanting effect.

Eva is in Spain, where she will decide one way or the other. She is standing on a dry-stone wall, brambles at her back and a cliff edge before her. Ten metres below, the water seethes over rocks. There is no beach here but this peninsula has scores of them, small and stony and empty. She has seen the words 'playa nudista' spray-painted somewhere on the rocks at every one she has been to. A local joke, she thinks. She took her bikini off once, but when she did it felt like everything was watching her: the trees, the birds, the advancing sea.

A freighter cuts south through the sun-silver water. Her destination lies north: a lighthouse on the headland, squat and brilliantly white. It is perhaps another three kilometres. It's barely 10 a.m. but the heat is powerful.

She is grateful for the wind gusting off the sea. She enjoys the way it snatches at her then just as suddenly lets her go.

Up close the white masonry of the lighthouse is less immaculate. Tapering stripes of rust run from the iron balustrade around the diamond-paned lantern room. The lantern flashes: two quick bursts every ten seconds. She counts twenty of these, and when she looks away her eyes carry a lurid afterimage. She goes into the dim, windowless gift shop and for a few seconds stands still, unable to see anything. She buys a postcard: an old black-and-white picture of the lighthouse.

Behind the lighthouse, in a hollow that shelters it from the worst of the wind, is an outdoor cafe. People are sitting in couples, trios and quartets at its trestle tables. She finds an empty table and orders a beer and a plate of squid from a waiter with drooping eyes, like a bloodhound's. She looks back along the length of her walk and to the north, beyond the cafe, where the Pyrenees end. The sky is a high, greyish blue. There are clouds out to sea. She finishes eating and lights a cigarette. She orders an espresso and takes out her guidebook, a tattered brick that covers all of Europe. It is old – it belonged to her mother – and has grown soft as a phone book from use. The pages are loose, and she has lost several regions in transit. Because of its age it is almost worthless as a source of information: disconnected telephone numbers, inaccurate maps, descriptions of restaurants and bars that closed down long ago. Nevertheless, its contents fascinate Eva. Opening it at random, the way she has done since she was a little girl, she finds herself in the Baltic. It has three gulfs, she reads: Bothnia, Finland and Riga. She looks at the map, the sea light grey, the land dark grey. The sun is at its peak. She lights another cigarette and flips the book's pages, their movement stirring the silver-grey flakes in the ashtray. She is somewhere in the Carpathians. She is in Provence. She is in Innsbruck. It is one of the pages the book likes to fall open to, as if prompting her. She looks at a black-and-white picture of grand old buildings lining a square festooned with sun umbrellas. Above the square looms a vast wall of wrinkled rock. The mountains are thickly forested on their lower slopes, blank white at their peaks. She feels the cold air gusting off them and blowing through the square, where she sits at a cafe waiting for . . . This is where her reverie breaks down; she is not sure who, or what, she is waiting for. The caption beneath the picture says: *Innsbruck, the sophisticated capital of the Alps*. She reads the brief description of the city, only half paying attention to words she has read many times before. Her fingers move across the map of Austria, tracing the thin, crooked lines of its rivers.

She walks back to Cadaqués by the same route she took to the lighthouse, on dusty trails that wind along the coastal ridges. She measures her pace because of the heat. The trail thins and she moves onto the verge of the winding road, away from the sea and the wind. Pebbles clatter across the tarmac, dislodged by her running shoes. She passes a barren field where breezeblock walls start and end at random, marking out patches of scrub or a few ragged sage bushes – their pepper and lemon scent infuses the still air. A van passes her, white, with a narrow ladder at the back. Its horn sounds, an irritated bleat swallowed by the hot air and the pulse of cicadas. Was that meant for her? She hears the tone of the engine change and she tenses, not wanting the van to stop here on the quiet road, but it is only shifting to a lower gear as the road rises.

Eva is hungry by the time she gets back. She has a glass of wine and a plate of ham on the shaded terrace of a small seafront bar, but the wine tastes sour and the meat, webbed with fat, sickens her. Her period is due, she thinks; maybe that's it. As she is leaving the bar a man, sitting alone, stands and inclines his head.

'Excuse me?' he says. He is English. Handsome, tall, fair, neatly dressed in white polo shirt and blue shorts.

Eva smiles weakly. She doesn't want to talk.

'You're English . . . ?' the man says. 'Speak English?'

'Swedish,' Eva says. 'But yes, I speak English. I live in England.'

'Right!' the man says, as if Eva has provided an answer he has long been looking for. 'Forgive me, I really don't want to intrude but I'll regret not asking; would you have dinner with me?' His eyes flash. He enjoys his boldness, she can tell.

'Thank you,' she says, smiling, 'that's nice of you, but I'm with someone.' She waves her left hand, even though she wears no rings.

The man smiles and nods, unembarrassed by the rejection. 'I'm very sorry I disturbed you,' he says.

She goes back to her hotel, showers, and sits with her book on the balcony: Moberg's *The Emigrants*, which she neglected to read at school and now feels she should know. But the pace is plodding and there is too much description. She drops the book to the tiles and closes her eyes. When she goes inside, the contrast between the bright day and the dim room makes it difficult to navigate. The brown and white bathroom fittings have turned a sickly green and yellow. She lies down on the bed and feels a breeze pass through the balcony doors. It makes the euros curled on her bedside table tremble. She falls asleep.

Hunger wakes her. The room is dark. She ate dinner at the hotel once before and promised herself she wouldn't do so again, but the nearest restaurant is a fifteen-minute walk and she is so tired from the hike that she doesn't want to go further than downstairs. It isn't only tiredness: part of her is worried about running into her English admirer.

Eva orders a tuna salad. Everything except the lettuce is tinned. The tuna is grey and heavily dressed with a jelly-like substance that tastes of sugar and margarine. If she hadn't been so fearful, she chides herself, she could have gone to the supermarket and eaten on the balcony: olives, a pepper, a sausage, a peach. The olives here look like tiny apples. As she tries to cut an artichoke heart it sags and fans out under her knife, its layers parting like the pages of a book. A clear fluid spills from it and spreads across her plate.

Realising she is hunched low over her meal, Eva un-curls and straightens her back. The light is low and yel-lowy, and her reflection in the window is murky: her skin is grey, her eyes pools of soot. She is sitting stiffly upright, clutching her knife and fork like weapons. The room around her is spectral. At the table beside her, drab and indistinct, she sees a couple. Are they staring at her? She hears a whisper and laughter and turns away from the window to look at them. They are young, twenty-some-things. Both tall, both slim. She hasn't seen them at break-fast or around the pool. The woman, her back to Eva, is wearing a bikini top, and the paleness of her skin suggests they are newly arrived. She hears snatches of their conver-

sation: 'the woman . . . the woman . . . that woman . . .'
It's her they mean. The young man laughs, but when his
eyes meet Eva's he stops. They are laughing at her dusty
trainers and her tired leggings, at her top that gathers at
the belly and her puffy eyes and table for one. Why are
the tables so close together? She could reach out and pull
the woman's blonde hair, yank her down across the table
and drag her fork across that long, white back. Or she
could use it on herself. Go up to her room, draw a bath,
numb her arms and puncture the white skin of her wrists.
White as that back. White as the belly of a fish. Caught
between her neighbours and her reflection, Eva looks
down at the table. I don't fucking care what they think,
she tells herself. Don't fucking care. Don't. Fucking. Care.
She stares at the remains of her salad: brown artichoke,
grey tuna, white lettuce stems. When the waiter comes to
take it away she waves him off. Until the couple beside
her are gone she will not move. She remains in her chair
as if turned to stone.

#

*Shut off from the rest of Yugoslavia by the rugged Dinaric
Alps, the Dalmatian coast is notable for its large number
of islands, coves and channels. The waters of the Adriatic are warm, salty and mostly shallow, with a maximum*

depth of 1000 metres. The coastline's climate is Mediter-
ranean. The soil is generally poor, but olives and grapes
flourish.

Earlier that summer Eva had flown from London to
Zagreb, then taken a train to Split. In Split she caught a
bus that travelled along the coast road to Dubrovnik. A
couple of hours into the journey the bus passed briefly
into Bosnia, and Eva held out her passport for inspection
by a border guard who didn't even look at it, just walked
up and down the aisle and sent them on their way with a
tired wave.

The last light was leaving the sky as the bus pulled into
Dubrovnik. Stepping down onto the tarmac Eva saw a red
digital display hanging from the bus terminal's canopy. It
alternated between time and temperature: 21:30, 21°C.
The place was swarming, and saturated in a fluorescence
that gave everything too much definition. Waiting in the
heat and fumes for the driver to open the luggage hatches,
Eva felt everything drop away from her, a sensation like
a plane hitting an air pocket. The busy scene around her
evaporated into uninterrupted white, and the sound of
voices, engines and announcements dwindled to a hiss.
She floated queasily, submersed. Then, as if propelled to
the surface, it all rushed back at her: the world returned.
She fell back and sat heavily on the kerb. She watched the
driver scrambling around inside the luggage hold, yank-

ing out the last few bags. His trousers had sagged. She read the words GOOD MAN repeating around the elastic band of his underwear.

The small tourist information office in the terminal was closed. Eva found a bench and pulled out her guidebook. She felt self-conscious, as if everyone walking past could see how indecisive she was being. On the bus journey she had circled some Old Town hotels on her map of the city, despite it being thirty years out of date. But whether they still existed or not she wanted to be somewhere quickly, right away, to shut out the lights and sleep for as long as she could. The thought of a taxi was intolerable. She found a listing for a hotel a short walk away, on Gruž Harbour. Standing in the overlit lobby she didn't pay attention to the price, just handed the receptionist her card.

The next morning, feeling stupid about her strange panic, she checked out and moved to a small hotel in the Old Town. In the afternoon she wandered the streets, unable to resist sliding her sandalled feet over their extraordinarily smooth flagstones. It was the way she had often walked when she was a child. 'Pick up your feet, Eva,' she heard her mum telling her.

Everywhere she went she seemed to be surrounded by tour groups, all following guides holding little flags with the name of their cruise ship on it. She made a game of avoiding them but she couldn't win, they were everywhere. That night, at a crowded outdoor bar on the fringe of rocks between the city walls and the sea, she met Josip.

'I buy you a drink?' he asked, and Eva said yes, she'd have a beer. Getting ready to go out she had pretended she was going to find somewhere low-key where she could have a drink and sit and read her book, but she had really wanted a place like this, with music and a young crowd. She had left the book in her room.

They spoke about the most basic things – what Dubrovnik was like, what London was like – but they made each other laugh. He looked like he was in his twenties, and Eva thought he might be ten or even fifteen years younger than her, but she didn't care.

'Dubrovnik is . . .' he said, pausing the way he often did midway through his sentence, carefully evaluating what to say next in a way Eva liked, '. . . is beautiful of course. But the life, the tourists. It doesn't always feel like a . . . *real* city.'

A cruise ship was leaving port, its hundreds of cabins lit gold. A few people around them catcalled. 'Tourists,' Eva said with disgust, giving the ship the finger. She laughed. She was drinking her third bottle of beer.

'They are leaving. That's good,' Josip said. There was a pause. 'Shall we leave, too?'

Standing alone in Josip's kitchen, restless with alcohol, Eva looked at his fridge door. A magnet in the shape of a bird clutched a postcard in its claws. On the postcard was a photograph of a church on a square with a fountain and arches. One side of the square was lined with brightly coloured houses. She plucked it from the bird's grip and turned it over. On the back there was scratchy handwriting in English:

Josip, I think of you. I am in Slovakia now wearing rain coat picking chestnuts. Markéta x

The legend on the card said 'Poprad, Slovensko'. Eva put it back and heard the toilet flush. Josip came into the kitchen, his face grave.

'You would like a beer?' he said.

'Yes.'

In bed, the darkness cut by a yellow stripe of streetlight falling through the shutters, Josip moved above her. She thought she could hear rain outside, but when she turned her head the noise stopped. She moved her hands from Josip's chest and gripped his hips and pushed him away.

'What's wrong?' Josip said, panting. He pressed against her hands a little, forcing her elbows down into the mattress. She pushed against him more firmly and squirmed towards the wall at the head of the bed, dragging him out of her.

'I'm sorry,' she said, 'I'm sorry.'

He told her it didn't matter. They lay in the dark not speaking. Then he asked her if she would like him to take her to Mljet. 'It is somewhere you would like to see.'

She thought he was sweet to ask, and that in the morning he would make an excuse and they would never see each other again.

#

North of Galway begins the vast, desolate landscape of Connemara, scoured by ice and strewn with rock.

Earlier that year, at the beginning of spring, she had rented a small cottage outside Clifden, in Connemara. Standing in the lee of a large hill, its back turned to the sea, the cottage looked over sloping fields divided by high stone walls. The bogs were humped with moss and heather and bedraggled sedges. Everything was dull, grey and green and brown, except for occasional sprays of yellow wildflowers that hung above the ground in little galaxies.

It rained all week, so hard that the mountains were never more than dark smears on the horizon. The firewood got wet. Rather than call the owner, whose phone number was printed on a laminated sheet of paper taped to the kitchen countertop, Eva spent most of the week mummified in blankets. A shivering mass, she paced the cottage's small rooms when she could no longer sit still. She jumped on the spot until she was breathless and warm. Sitting in a large, lumpy armchair she read novels from the cottage's collection: Ian Rankin, John Buchan, Pat Barker. She read them all at once, switching between them whenever she felt like a change. Characters and events slipped from one book into another, creating a new, incoherent but exciting story. She didn't cook, only drank mug after mug of tomato soup with buttered white bread.

At last one morning the rain stopped and a lance of sun pierced the front of the house. Light spilled down the hillside. Eva pulled on walking boots, tied a jumper around her waist and almost ran from the house. The beach was no distance. She marched over the springy, uneven ground. The sedges brushed her jeans, leaving dark slashes. The rain resumed, sudden as a tap, and Eva's stride became a trudge. She passed a line of sodden, defeated hazels. Rocks and seaweed lay scattered on the beach. Water bubbled up around her footsteps in the sand. The beach was on an inlet, and on the opposite shore two white ponies stood on the hillside, motionless in the rain. Their manes hung in lank corkscrews.

She turned a circle on the shore. On a nearby hill she saw some kind of monument, a black wing pointing at the sky. She saw the rise that hid her cottage. Little mouths opened and closed on the surface of the water, the rain falling into them. The sand darkened. She could just walk in. The thought, small and simple, arrived like a bird alighting on a branch. She turned and walked quickly back to the cottage.

In the living room, wrapped in towels, she looked at a framed photograph of the peat bogs in summer. The land was scored with dark lines where the turf had been cut. The harvested sods lay beside the trenches in small black stooks, drying in the sun. She thought of the coldness of the water, and gripped the towels more tightly around her.

The next day a cat scratched at her door and she fed it tuna from a can she found at the back of a cupboard. It stayed. They ate together and stared out of the window. She read from her guide to Europe, and the cat dragged its cheek along the corner of the book's spine. She fell asleep with the book in her lap and woke up in the thick-shadowed dusk, overwarm and confused. At night there was a light pressure at her back, and she felt as much as heard the rich thrum of the cat's purr. After three days it disappeared. Outside the windows the rain stood in solid silver walls.

\#

Away from the shore, the warren of backstreets provides interesting options for more discerning diners.

It is on one of the steep, undulating streets away from the seafront that Eva sees him again, the man who asked her to dinner. The narrow, shadowy street is residential; there is no helpful shop to slip into.

He holds up a hand in greeting as they near one another. He is wearing the same clothes as before but in different colours: grey polo, white shorts.

'Hello.' Eva smiles, not intending to stop, but the man moves into her path.

'Sorry,' he says, sounding casual. 'I just wanted to say something. You mind?'

She shakes her head. An overweight Spanish woman in black skirt and shirt seesaws past, a squeaking yellow bucket in her hand.

'I've seen you wandering all around here,' the man says, smiling in a way that suggests bemusement rather than happiness. 'I know you aren't with anyone. Look, that sounds . . .' He holds his hands up, palms out. 'I have no problem with you not wanting to have dinner with me, but I asked politely and I would have appreciated an honest answer.'

She wants to close her eyes and wish him away. 'I'm sorry,' she says. 'It was rude of me. I've been unwell. I *am* unwell.' She is surprised to hear herself say the words.

'I'm sorry. What's wrong?'

At this new impertinence Eva, whose eyes had dropped

to the cobbles at her feet, looks up. Anger sparks inside her. 'It's personal. I don't want to talk about it.' After she has spoken she feels, for just a moment, that he will hit her.

He flaps his hand as if batting a fly. 'You're rude,' he says, and walks past her.

She takes a few steps in the opposite direction before she stops and turns. 'You have no right!' she shouts after him. 'I am unwell!'

He doesn't turn, only makes a mouth of one hand and opens and closes it.

'You have no fucking right,' she says, but not loud enough for him to hear. Looking around, she sees a cobble dislodged from its bed. She reaches for it, pulls back her arm and hurls it at the man. It lands beside him and skitters down the street. He turns, incredulous. 'You're a fucking madwoman!' he shouts. He steps towards her and stops. He turns, first to his right then to his left, flexing his hands into fists then blades, fists then blades. Eva cannot move. Her breath is fast and thin. If he comes closer, she thinks, I need to run.

She turns and walks, the adrenaline making her feet stutter against the cobbles. She knows she will replay this encounter for days, for weeks. She turns into an alleyway that heads steeply downhill. A cat with matted fur and a chewed ear slides past her with a wary flick of its head.

She must escape the tangle of these small streets. She must reach the sea.

#

Extensively rebuilt following the heavy bombing it suffered during World War Two, Le Havre has struggled to return to its position among France's main cargo ports. The city remains busy with ferry traffic to Britain and Ireland, however, and it is worth some exploration, if only on the way to somewhere else.

As soon as she returned from Ireland, Eva made plans to go away again. She didn't want to be in her flat, which still felt like a temporary residence two years after she moved in. Half of her things were still in boxes. She had moved around after she left Sweden: France, Milan, a suburb of Washington DC. She has been in London for the last ten years, not because she likes it more than anywhere else but because it was where inertia set in. More and more often, though, she found she didn't want to be walking its familiar, dreary streets. She had a two-week booking at an advertising agency in Hammersmith, a job she virtually slept through. She worked with her headphones on, and communicated as much as she could get away with by email. The work, retouching photographs for a series of brochures, was simple, but what she supplied was barely satisfactory and she knew they wouldn't use her again.

The day she finished, a Wednesday, she got on a train at Waterloo and took an overnight ferry across a flat Channel from Portsmouth to Le Havre. When she arrived her hotel room wasn't ready, so she left her luggage and said she'd be back in the afternoon. She stopped at a cafe for coffee and a pastry. It was years since she had been in France, the first place she had gone when she left Sweden for good. She had worked as a waitress in a hotel outside Poitiers. It had been a strange time, not least because she didn't know the language very well. She made one real friend, a sous-chef called Denis. He had no Swedish and very little English, but they both loved the Cure and when all else failed they would recite song titles back and forth: 'All Cats Are Grey', 'Sinking', 'Three Imaginary Boys'. They liked the saddest songs best. Denis was a few years older, with a wife and young son. They had promised to keep in touch but their letters had petered out. She hadn't thought about him for a long time. Did he remember her?

In the enormous space of Avenue Foch trams and a stream of cars moved past. Long modernist blocks loomed. There were few pedestrians. The sky was white-grey and a cold breeze came from the sea, which lay at the end of the avenue. Standing at a crossing her eyes filled with tears, so completely that for an instant she couldn't see. Spasms hit her body. She wanted to wipe the tears out of her eyes, but couldn't lift her arms. There had been episodes like this after her mum died. The sensation, so long forgotten, was instantly familiar. She felt ridiculous, but she couldn't move. She was a tree in the wind, powerless to do anything but endure. Another spasm went through her and she thought she might be sick. She heard a voice and lifted her head towards the sound.

Her vision began to make sense again. She saw her own face, stricken and doubled: her reflection in the lenses of a large pair of sunglasses worn by a middle-aged woman in a long black coat. 'Est-ce que vous vous sentez bien?' The woman's mouth was a rich red, small and cruel, but her voice was consoling. She reached out and held Eva's wrist. 'You speak English?' she said. 'You are OK?'

'Yes,' Eva said and smiled even as another sob came out of her. The woman drew a tissue from her handbag. Eva nodded thanks. She blew her nose and took a deep breath. It had passed. Its ferocity had scared her. She asked the woman if there was a church nearby. She needed quiet.

'Yes,' the woman said. 'Turn left, walk straight. Saint-Joseph. You will see it. It is . . .' She held her hands diagonally apart to show the scale, but to Eva it looked, also, as if she were asking for a skewed hug. The gesture was childlike, at odds with her severe appearance.

'Thank you,' Eva said. 'You've been very kind.'

'You are welcome,' the woman said slowly, gravely nodding her head and stiffening her body, as if she might salute.

Saint-Joseph was concrete and immense. Its blocky edifice supported an octagonal spire that looked more like a scale model of a skyscraper than a church tower. The vast interior was as hushed as Eva had hoped. It was, perhaps, even empty: she couldn't see anyone else. The noise of the street outside was very faint. Massive, undressed concrete pillars rose in groups of four, lashed together by horizontal crosses. Spotlights blanched the grey pillars yellow-white. There weren't any pews, just rows of theatre-like seats upholstered in cream fabric. Eva found the empty chairs eerie in their blankness. She preferred to look at the church's windows, fitted with thousands of small panes of stained glass: blue, yellow, orange and green, although on that sunless day the panes were dull, dead. Eva walked around a railing that separated the altar from the congregation and stood beneath the octagonal tower. She didn't know what she was doing there. She didn't know what she was doing in France.

'What am I doing in France?' she said out loud. She repeated it, then repeated it again, placing the stress on different words in turn. '*What* am I doing in France? What *am* I doing in France? What am *I* doing in France?' She asked herself once more and felt the ground quiver.

She fell back against the railing and lifted her head. The tower's uniform sections of concrete and glass sped away from her, their diminishing perspective pulling her eye towards what looked like a black aperture at its apex. This is what a bullet must feel like, she thought, just before it gets shot from the barrel.

Eva went back to the hotel and told the manager she wouldn't need the room.

'You stay somewhere else?' He sounded jealous.

'I have to leave,' she said. 'I have to go home.'

'But you are only arrived.'

'Yes. I have to leave today.'

On the late-afternoon ferry Eva stood on deck and looked back at the city through a soft but very cold rain. She saw a shining light and realised, as the ferry began lurching across bigger waves, that she was looking at the spire of Saint-Joseph. The cross, thrust high above the city, shone out. She continued to stare, no longer seeing. The next time she noticed what she was looking at, there was only the churning sea.

She remembered that crossing on the catamaran to Mljet. Josip had surprised her by honouring his promise. She tried to explain what happened the night before, but he lifted his hand to indicate that she didn't need to. Their legs were touching, and shook lightly with the engine's vibration. *Of all the Adriatic islands*, Eva read in her guidebook, *Mljet might be the most seductive*. From the harbour they took a taxi, and Josip showed her the cave where Calypso kept Odysseus, broken ground sloping down to it. Alone, close to the cave's mouth, Josip stood behind Eva and pressed his erection against her back. She leaned back slightly, and his arms snaked around her. He cupped her breasts and squeezed. She squirmed and he continued to press, until finally they were dropped into a sort of crouch, like skiers. His wrists were in her armpits, and his elbows pressed into the top of her tensed thighs. The sea stretched out in front of her. His shallow breaths were sour with tobacco.

'Let's go closer,' she said.

He straightened up immediately and stepped away from her. He seemed angry. 'Come,' he said, as if ending a dispute, 'I will show you.'

That night they ate at an open-air trattoria, sitting on a stone terrace set with white plastic chairs and tables. Eva's hunger was enormous. She drank a carafe of white wine – Mljet wine, Josip told her with pride as he filled her glass – and started another before their food arrived. She called for schnapps when their main courses came. 'To our meeting!' she said, cracking her glass against his. She tried to teach him 'Helan Går', a drinking song, but he couldn't follow the words. With her coffee she drank an oily, abrasive grappa.

There was a dancefloor below the terrace, and a band playing folk songs and pop. Josip stared at her intently as they danced. He looked as if he wanted to scold her and was searching for the words to express his anger. Because of what happened at the cave? Let him stew, Eva thought. She was determined to have fun tonight. She was surprised at how lightly he moved. He became less angular when he danced. He moved his hips. She wanted to have sex with him. She pictured the scene from the afternoon as if she had been someone else standing at the cave's mouth, watching them fuck: she half-crouching, he behind her with brow creased, the same furious look on his face as now, pressing himself further and further inside her.

The dancefloor had filled. Turning her back, Eva danced into Josip. She pulled his arms around her waist. She ground against him and lifted his hands towards her breasts, but when he realised what she was doing he resisted, and she couldn't move them any more. The music's tempo increased and her movements grew wilder. She collided with other dancers. She piled her hair on top of her head and left her hands buried in it as she thrashed her head from side to side. She ground against him more firmly still and colours sprayed across her closed eyes as the band played louder, faster. The accordion reminded her of fairgrounds. The sound of it made her feel sick.

'Let's sit down,' she said.

Back from the dancefloor stood a grove of tall pines. White chairs, scattered in twos and threes between the trees, almost glowed in the night. The darkness throbbed with the din of cicadas. Eva could smell the trees, their needles soft beneath her sandals. She sat down, and felt a layer of gritty dust against her legs. Josip lit a cigarette.

'Can I have one of those?' she said. He pulled the packet from his shirt pocket and pushed up the lid with his thumb. She hadn't smoked in many years and the flavour brought back the first time she tried, in a schoolfriend's garden shed. The shed had smelled of creosote, motor oil and pine resin. The smoke made her lightheaded. Her queasiness gone, she stretched with pleasure. Her eyes were getting used to the dark, and the trees' bark seemed to shine. It was patterned: grey scales, dagger-shaped, repeated over and over, with darker channels between them. She reached out and gripped one of the scales. The wood was soft, and came off the tree very easily. 'Why do you look like that when you dance?' she asked, waving the piece of bark slowly like a fan.

'Look like what?' Josip said.

'Angry,' she said.

'I look angry?'

'Yes. Like—' She pulled a face like his, only more grotesque: brows low and lips in a tight pout.

'Like what?'

'Like that. I just did it.' It was too dark for him to see, of course. She could only make out the shifting glint of his eyes.

'When I dance I concentrate,' he said. 'Dancing is not easy.'

'What else do you do that requires such concentration?' She heard her words slur. He was silent. This wasn't what she wanted. She wanted to be playful, and for Josip to be playful in response, and for this lightness to be effortless and to last and last, but he was silent. She threw the bark at him and it hit his chin and fell onto his chest. He left it there and didn't say anything. 'Then you say . . .' she prompted, smiling. He was silent. The band was playing something slow now, and deeper in the darkness, above the insect hiss, a man's voice spoke sharply. He spoke for a long time, and when he finally stopped there was no reply.

#

The village follows the line of a half-dozen small coves. At points along the street beside the water's edge there is no railing, so watch your step.

It is Eva's last day in Cadaqués. She wakes early and takes a pastry and coffee onto the hotel terrace. It is shaded at this hour, and the chairs and tables are damp from the rain that fell in the night. She hears talk drifting down from the balconies above, German, French and English voices making plans for the day. Above the sound of a protesting child a woman repeats, 'Arrêt, arrêt, arrêt,' calmly but relentlessly.

When she has packed, Eva takes the books she brought with her down to a bookcase in the TV lounge. *The Emigrants*, which she will never finish, and two thrillers she didn't even begin. She used to read all the time. Proper books. She had enjoyed it more than anything, seeing all the things a life might hold. A printed sign stuck to the top of the bookcase reads *Biblioteca | Bibliothèque | Library*. She slips her books, pristine, between creased, water-curled neighbours.

She takes a final walk to the village, where she will have lunch before leaving. The day is hot. The sun presses itself into her. On a track away from the road, a shortcut she has found, she bends to study the desiccated corpse of an octopus. Only when she is on her haunches does she realise it is a twisted length of underwear elastic, caked in dust and dirt.

It is the weekend and the village is busier than she has seen it, filled with day-trippers and promenading families. Surprised by the crowds around the main plaza, facing the sea, Eva leans against a telegraph pole to watch people come and go. On the junction box beside her is a photocopied flyer, curled at the edges, for a recital by a Japanese pianist. A round sticker has been placed over the pianist's face: *¡Si, Independència!* in white on red. She has seen waiters and shopkeepers wearing the same badge. On the plaza a band begins to play and people, locals, dance in a ring, joining hands and holding them aloft. Eva turns and continues walking around the bay, towards its quieter northern tip.

Ahead of her a group of tourists are standing with hands on hips, apparently stunned by the sun and sea. One of them says something in German and points. The others stare at the sea and nod, as if it were speaking to them. A tall woman says something about 'luft'. Air. The woman's companions smile and take exaggerated, snorting breaths. Eva feels a sudden love for them. She wants to stand among them and admire the water and breathe the air. She wants to point at the trees, and the cliffs, and the sun.

But the group moves on, leaving Eva alone. She looks out to sea and knows that the horizon is only the limit of her vision: the water goes on for endless miles. Dizzy, she bends to grasp the hot, smooth slate of the promenade wall. She hangs her head down and laughs. In the water below her, children are paddling and pulling starfish from rocks. A father is teaching his son to snorkel and the child's legs thrash, yellow flippers on his feet. Above them, on a clear blue day, a woman is hanging on for her life, her head down and her hair falling towards the pavement. Yesterday she stood screaming in the street. She thought about slitting her wrists. She stares along the length of herself, at her breasts and belly, at her hips and thighs. The sun warms her nape. A soft breeze, like a breath, dabs her cheek. She came here to decide, and she has decided. She will go to Innsbruck, sit on the square and feel the wind that comes down from the mountains. There is a river there; she has traced its course with her finger. It runs on to meet the Danube, mingles, separates, and is something else completely by the time it empties into the sea.

THE HAVÄNG DOLMEN

Several months ago, while travelling in Sweden, I experienced something I have given up trying to explain. In fact, since it happened I have tried to push it as far from my mind as possible. But yesterday afternoon, searching for an errant set of keys, I found, nestled deep in a coat pocket, an acorn that I plucked from its cap in the forest beneath the fortress of Stenshuvud. Then it was smooth and green, but now it is tawny, and ribbed like a little barrel. You wouldn't know it was the same acorn I picked on a whim, but holding it I felt again the compulsion that propelled me, at the end of that strange day, into the burial chamber at Haväng.

It was the end of September. I was attending a three-day conference in Lund. It finished early on a Friday afternoon, and with the weekend ahead of me, and nothing to hurry back to London for, I elected to stay. My colleagues recommended some sites – Iron and Stone Age, neither eras of particular interest to me, but I thought why not. The only one I had heard of was Ale's Stones, Sweden's Stonehenge, built on a clifftop above the Baltic in the shape of a great ship.

I had presented a paper at the conference, 'Digging Deeper: On the Aetiology of Archaeological Belief'. It was good work, and I was excited about the presentation, but the few people who turned up lacked the ability to grasp even the simplest of the points I was making. It was a blessing when it was all over and I could leave Lund. I needed some time away from people.

Escaping the rush-hour traffic I drove my hire car east on Riksväg 11 to Simrishamn, a small fishing village on the eastern coast of Skåne, Sweden's southernmost county. I drove between gently sloping hills, past apple orchards, and beside the ruffled green seas of sugar beet fields. The weather swung rapidly, as it had all week, between showers and sun.

Approaching Simrishamn on the coastal road I saw a rainbow springing from the sea. I pulled over and got out of the car to admire it. It arced from the water and disappeared into a low, dark cloud. Its bands had an unusual solidity. The wind gusted, and the grey sea was ridged like a tilled field. I felt a long way from the stuffy rooms and obtuse debates of Lund.

I checked into a small hotel a short walk from the harbour. I thought the holiday season was over, but in fact I only managed to get a room because of a late cancellation: the receptionist told me an apple festival, one of the locality's most significant annual events, was taking place in the nearby town of Kivik.

Finding a small fridge in my room, I decided to get supplies and make the following day's lunch. The hotel might have been full, but I didn't see anyone in its corridors. The town also seemed largely deserted. Everyone was in Kivik, I supposed, worshipping the apple. The wind was blowing less forcefully now, but the sun had also faded. It was wet and warm, and the light had a greenish cast. Near the harbour the buildings were old and low, half-timbered, divided by narrow lanes and small cobbled squares. Further back from the shore the stock ceded to concrete and brick modernity, as typical as it was ugly.

I bought bread, meat, cheese and two blood-red apples. As I was queuing to pay I noticed a commotion by the entrance; a boy, seemingly drunk, was taunting shoppers as they passed. He accosted me, too, as I exited. He didn't touch me, but stood in my way so that I was forced to stop. We faced each other. He was perhaps eighteen or so, with very short hair, an upturned nose, and blue eyes that, despite his unsteadiness, were extraordinarily clear and penetrating. His face reminded me of someone – I couldn't place whom, but I had the sense it was someone I hadn't thought about for a long time. In that moment, as he stared at me, I felt certain he was about to speak my name. What came out of his mouth instead was no less strange: a series of drawn-out screeches, aggressive and birdlike. I tried to move past him but he shifted position to block me, continuing to emit the aggravating noise. His lips were drawn back from his brown teeth; he reeked of alcohol and tobacco. Behind him, on the short flight of steps leading up to the street, a fat, vacant-looking girl sat smoking. Looking at me she spoke rapidly in Swedish, giggling as the shrieks grew even louder. Shoppers were hurrying past, not wanting to get involved. The concrete porch we were standing in felt as though it were shrinking, pushing me, the boy and the girl closer and closer together. Beginning to panic, I forced my way past the boy and hurried away, not stopping until I was back at my hotel. His screeches rang in my ears long after I had left him behind.

I made sandwiches and put them in the fridge ready for the next day's expedition. I had some food left over and considered having it for dinner, but my room felt too confining. I walked through the still-deserted streets in the direction of the harbour.

I hadn't been walking long before I found a restaurant with a name that called to me: Cimbris. It was familiar, I realised, from the conference. Someone had spoken about the Cimbri, an Iron Age tribe that spread from Jutland. They harassed the Romans, even getting as far as Italy at one point, then disappeared from history the way tribes, even entire civilisations, sometimes do, the archaeological record providing no answer to why they should have dropped off the face of the earth.

The restaurant was busy, and I was stuck in a corner at a small, wobbly table on the threshold of the men's toilet. I thought about complaining, but my waitress was so thuggish I didn't want to interact with her any more than I had to. The food was surprisingly good, though: grilled plaice in a butter sauce, and boiled potatoes dressed with dill. For dessert, fried apples with whipped cream: the surplus, I presumed, from the nearby festival.

After dinner I crossed the street to the harbour. Lamps cast pools of yellow light along the jetties. The air was cool, and the water so still that every boat had a perfect double hanging from its hull. As I wandered, enjoying having the harbour entirely to myself, I realised I wasn't in fact alone: a figure, tall and thin, was standing on the seawall and looking out over the black water. I considered approaching him. There was no one else around, nor any movement in the town at our backs, nor even – or so it seemed for a few moments – any sound from the invisible sea. Where was the screaming boy now? The thought of him prowling the streets unsettled me, and instead of joining the watcher on the seawall I hurried to my hotel, half expecting to hear that uncanny shriek again. In fact I walked back in perfect solitude, but in my room, lying in the dark and beginning to slip into sleep, I unexpectedly heard the excited shouts of children from somewhere in the nearby streets.

I set off early the next morning. The day was bright, the streets still and peaceful. First I would visit the remains of an Iron Age fort on the headland at Stenshuvud, then pass through Kivik on my way up the coast to the Haväng Dolmen.

When I arrived at Stenshuvud the visitor centre was shut up and silent. Through the trees the white sea dazzled, but despite the sun's brightness there was no warmth in the air. The walk up to the fort began in a low, uneven pasture where sheep grazed. The churned ground was spongy underfoot, and at its lowest points was more sea than soil. Skirting muddy pools I thought of a lecture I had attended in Lund, more to fill time than anything else, about the Iron Age bodies found in bogs across northern Europe. Tollund Man was found in the Jutland Peninsula, home of the Cimbri, and was so well preserved that police mistook him for the victim in an unsolved murder case. Inside his stomach they found traces of the gruel he had eaten before he died. The lecturer, a Dutchwoman, concentrated mostly on the scientific methods used during the examinations and subsequent re-examinations of these finds, but she wasn't a gifted speaker, and it was only when she began showing pictures of the remains and describing how these men had died – some of this new to me, some half-remembered from undergraduate studies – that she won my full attention. Tollund Man had been hanged. Grauballe Man, another Jutlander, had his throat slashed. Lindow Man was strangled, received a double fracture of the skull, and had his jugular sliced. Clonycavan Man's head was split open with a stone axe. Arms and a torso appeared on the screen, purplish-red and wrinkled as a dried chilli. This was Old Croghan Man. In her monotone the lecturer recited the details of the overkill this young, unusually tall man had suffered: he was bound with hazel branches threaded through the skin of his upper arms, his nipples were snipped off, he was stabbed in the chest, stabbed in the neck, decapitated, and cut in half. 'Somehow,' she said, her voice thickening with rehearsed mirth, 'these wounds proved fatal.'

I stepped over a wooden stile and entered the beech forest that climbed towards the fort. The light beneath the trees was tea-coloured, the air cool, which I was glad of as the ground began to steepen. Stenshuvud is an outcrop rising a hundred metres above the sea, and my breathing was laboured by the time I broke free of the trees and felt the soft earth of the forest floor give way to rock.

The fort's remains, spread over three small peaks, were scant, but it was easy to see how well chosen it had been as a stronghold. From here you could keep watch over your entire surroundings. The first peak faced south, where heathland studded with junipers stretched to sand flats and, beyond, the sea; the second east, where bluffs dropped sharply to the water; the third looked back to the interior, down a creased and thickly forested valley.

This was the route I chose for my descent. Berry-like clusters of sheep droppings lay in mounds. Heather writhed across the ground. A regal oak stood heavy with plump acorns: green, orange and brown. I slipped one from its cap with a gentle tug. When I was a young child our next-door neighbour, a kind Welshman who whistled constantly through nervous habit, gave me an acorn he had taken from the grounds of Windsor Castle. My mother helped me plant it in the back garden, and from then on that little patch of ground was thought of as belonging to me. Over the years the oak grew to twice my height. When I was older, and I needed to move home for a period of time, I sat beneath it every day, telling it things I wasn't able to tell other people.

The acorn rested in my hand, smooth and apple-green. I rolled it between my fingers, deeply pleased by its shape and texture. At some point my old tree was stricken by a fungus and chopped down. My mother didn't tell me until after it was done. Now just a mossy stump is left. The fungus is still alive somewhere down in the roots; my mother tells me she scrapes it off when it pushes through the cracked surface of the wood.

I tucked the acorn away and walked on. My water bottle, half full, gulped in my pocket at every step. I heard chestnuts rattling through branches as they fell to the ground. On this side of the hill, where the beeches weren't dominant enough to block all the sunlight, the undergrowth was thicker and there were more signs of life. Stepping over a huge slug lying flat across the path, I heard a thrashing off in the distance. I stopped to listen and the sound ceased, but I had the sense that someone was very close by. I turned, thinking I'd see a fellow walker somewhere behind me. There was no one there. But turning again I did see someone, perhaps thirty feet ahead, part-screened by leaves and branches. They were tall, and seemed to be standing slowly from a kneeling position. 'Hey!' I called. There was no reply. I started towards the figure, which was still rising – now it seemed impossibly tall, perhaps twice my height. I had halved the distance between us when I heard something rushing at me from my left.

'Ursäkta!' a man cried as he sprinted past, almost knocking me to the ground.

'Idiot!' I shouted, but the runner had already disappeared among the trees. I turned back, but on the spot where I thought my watcher had stood I found nothing except bushes and a pile of dead branches.

By the time I reached Kivik I was hungry and the roads were crowded. Trapped in a slow-moving line of traffic, I crawled past the Kungagraven. In Lund, having coffee after a morning session, a Bronze Age specialist had stood too close and excitedly briefed me on 'the largest circular burial site in Sweden'. He had halitosis, and his enthusiasm for barrows was something I couldn't share, not when he stood breathing on me, and not as I stared from the car at a large, low mound of grey stones.

I rolled slowly past a group of boys sitting on the fence dividing the road from the field in which the Kungagraven lay. They were passing a bottle back and forth and shouting things at the cars, goading one another to be ever more outrageous. They seemed possessed by a hectic energy, and the violence of their laughter made me uneasy. It was then that I realised who the boy at the supermarket had looked like. Guillaume. I met him in France, on a family holiday when I was a child. He was short and muscular, like an acrobat, and had – just like that strange boy in Simrishamn – the most piercing blue eyes. I hadn't thought of him for years, but now his face hung before me as I listened to the boys' malicious laughter. They were like animals.

I had planned to eat my lunch in Kivik, but it looked unbearable. From the main road all the way down to the harbour the streets were thronged with festival-goers drinking cider and carrying sacks of apples. They clogged the pavements and spilled onto the road, braying and grinning like morons. I decided to head straight for Haväng, another ten kilometres up the coast.

I heard a crow's loud complaint as I got out of the car. The empty car park faced a grassy field inhabited by a few black and chestnut mares. The nearby sea was out of sight and silent. I closed my eyes and absorbed the quietness.

At the edge of the car park stood a cafe, which was closed. Beside it there was a small cement toilet block. Inside the men's a flickering tube spat yellow light on the damp cement floor and the dirty porcelain of the sink and urinal. A sodden, dissolving mass of toilet paper stood on the ledge of the sink. Barnacles of rust had formed on the taps. There was a single cubicle, which I was surprised to see was occupied. As I urinated I heard someone shifting on the toilet seat. For the second time that day I felt watched. I turned and looked at the small gap between the base of the cubicle and the floor, half expecting to see a face glaring out at me. I had an urge to go down on my knees and peer under, to see at least the shoes of whoever was in there. I went to the sink, but having my back to the cubicle made me almost shake with fear. I yanked open the door and threw myself outside.

There, my uneasiness instantly became laughable. The sun was shining, and now there was even some heat in the day. Realising how hungry I was, I decided to walk down to the beach and eat my lunch before visiting the dolmen.

I passed through a gate, walked up a short rise and from its crest saw the sea. A duckboard path sloped down to the beach, cutting across tussocky grass. I saw white, brown and yellow mushrooms bursting from cowpats, clumps of buttercups, and small networks of a blue flower I didn't recognise. When I was a child and we went on walks my mother, a woman who never wasted words, would recite the names of the trees and flowers we saw. The way she spoke made them sound like the words to a spell.

At the border between grass and sand stood a large concrete pillbox built into the bank, so I could walk directly onto its roof from the grass. It probably dated from the early years of the Cold War. The thickly littered steps leading down to its interior announced its dereliction. Beer bottles, plastic bags, crisp packets, fragments of wood and metal: the archaeological record in waiting. I sat on the edge of the concrete roof, my legs dangling. Sun and shadow alternated at speed. The ocean was flat and the beach was empty of people. Silver water lapped at the floury white sand. I ate my sandwiches slowly, lulled by the gentle sound of the waves and the drone of insects. The dolmen was somewhere behind me, but I didn't want to look at it yet. I wanted to save it. To my right, above a small pine wood, a dark, cracked cloud seemed to hold the sun prisoner: fissures in the cloud glowed with brilliant light.

I ate an apple and watched the currents show as zigzagging lines in the water. Scrolls of cloud receded to the horizon. I thought of the pillbox I was sitting on, and Stenshuvud, and the millennium that separated them: structures erected at the edge of things, repelling invaders. But our defences are always overrun eventually, by time if by nothing else. I decided I wouldn't go to the dolmen yet. I would walk along the beach then climb the low cliffs to the sloping grasslands above. They would carry me back down to the site.

I put the litter from my lunch in my knapsack and descended from the pillbox. Gulls launched themselves from the trees edging the beach and patrolled the sea in shallow parabolas. Sand flies flickered at my feet. Before two black wooden boathouses, their doors and windows sealed, I passed a large patch of burned straw, the remains of a beach fire. A little further on, climbing over some rocks, I slipped and sliced open the side of my hand on a jagged piece of granite. The wound wasn't so deep, but enough blood continued to well from it that I needed to staunch it: looking back I saw a line of dark spots running alongside my footsteps.

I sat down amid the exposed roots of a chestnut tree, its split, spiked pods littering the sand around me. I took a lightweight scarf from my knapsack and knotted it as tightly as I could around my hand. As I did so I felt, for the third time that day, that someone was watching me. As I looked around, confirming I was utterly alone, I dug the fingers of my good hand into the powdery sand. Dry and fine on the surface, it was dense and cold beneath.

Just before I left the beach, beside a steep track up the cliff that would allow me to double back towards the dolmen, I was confronted by a strange totem. It was a section of birch trunk embedded in the sand, its white bark mostly stripped away by the salt air. Halfway up the trunk a small branch reached out from it like a withered arm. The remains of an emerald-green net hung from the end of the branch. At the top of the trunk someone had wound a mass of white and yellow rope that had an unpleasant resemblance to human hair. Its frayed ends shifted in the breeze. Beneath the hair a crude face had been cut and scorched into the wood, its round eyes and slot mouth giving it a hateful, imbecilic expression. It stared back down the beach the way I'd come. Maybe this was my mystery watcher, I thought, and felt a fury rise up in me. I took up a length of driftwood and used it as a cudgel, thrashing at the totem until it lay in fragments on the sand.

Breathing hard, I climbed the path up to the grasslands. In the far distance, to the north, I could just make out a family: a woman, a child and a man. They were walking

away from me. There was no one else. My only companions were sheep, grazing at a distance from one another
on the ground sloping down to the dolmen.

At the edge of the site stood an information panel, an-
gled like a lectern. *The Haväng Dolmen, five thousand
years old, was uncovered by storms in 1843.* I didn't read
any more; I was impatient to explore the site for myself.
I skirted the square of jagged stones that marked the dolmen's perimeter, the grass around them springy, cropped,
and dotted with rabbit droppings. At the centre of the
site, an enormous porphyry capstone rested on several smaller stones to form a grave chamber six feet long,
four wide and three high. The chamber stood open on the
seaward side like a waiting mouth. A large red admiral
swirled past. I felt the lightness of being far from home,
the pleasure and terror of being free to do as I liked. No
one knew that I was here. No one would know if I didn't
return. I felt faint, and put my hand out to balance myself.
My cut hand throbbed against the perimeter stone, coated in flaking grey lichen. It was then that the feeling took
hold: a keen urge, a need, to lie within the burial chamber.
I scrambled towards its mouth, got down and squirmed
inside on my belly.

Once I was in as far as I could go, I twisted onto my
back. My clothes had ridden up, and the small of my back
pressed against the icy sand of the chamber floor. Look-

ing out between my feet, which lay outside the chamber still, I saw a strip of green grass and a grey band of sea. I dropped my head back into the sand. I looked up at the base of the capstone, streaked black and copper red. I reached out my hand and pressed it against the frigid rock, smooth against my palm.

I felt a deep tiredness seep through me. As the walls of stone closed in I shut my eyes. I heard the sea in the distance. I saw a cave mouth, and darkness streaming from it. Guillaume was beside me, I could feel the nearness of his body. I was ten again, on holiday in the south of France. He was a few years older, leader of a gang of local kids. He was fearless. I saw him on the beach, devising games, issuing orders, leaping about in the water. I thought he was magnificent, and as soon as he spoke to me I became his most loyal disciple. I followed him everywhere, to the surprise and relief of my parents: now I wouldn't be a burden to them.

On our last day together Guillaume and the others showed me a large cave you could swim into, just around from the little bay that had briefly been our kingdom. The cave's entrance was a shallow arch. At high tide, Guillaume said, it was all underwater. Inside, in the half-darkness, our cries merged into a ringing echo. The cave's entrance was a burning eye. Ripples in the water glided in golden ribbons across the stone above our heads.

My friends – I still thought they were my friends – showed me a ledge at the back of the cave where you could sit and hang your legs in the water. Guillaume pulled himself onto it and hauled me up beside him. The others stayed in the water. Guillaume showed me a passageway leading back into the rock. He told me that beyond this passageway lay another cave the others hadn't seen, one he wanted to share only with me. Gesturing towards the narrow crack in the rock, he said I should go first. I eagerly complied, but after just a couple of steps I had to turn my body sideways, and after only a little more progress squeezing myself through the passage I was stuck fast. I couldn't even turn my head to ask for help, so I shouted back to Guillaume. I heard him laugh at me. There was the splash of a body returning to the water, and someone shouted, 'Bye, English!' There was more laughter, then only the sound of water sloshing in the empty cave.

I was helpless. For a long time I did nothing but cry. Eventually, desperate, I began wrenching my body forward and back against the rock. I felt my skin tearing, but still I wasn't free. I remember feeling each pump of my heart, how it seemed to squeeze against the rock. I believed what Guillaume had said about the cave being underwater at high tide. I was convinced I was going to drown. I could see my corpse stuck there, its hair waving in the water. Lying in the burial chamber, returned to that narrow space between those pinning walls, I felt the certainty of nearing death.

I opened my eyes and saw the capstone above me. I was very cold. I heard the crashing of waves from the beach below. I scrambled between capstone and sand, digging my heels into the ground to help lever myself out, but I couldn't move. I felt as though the life was being crushed out of me. I closed my eyes and tried to breathe, and felt a scatter of rain on my face. I looked down at the entrance to the dolmen and saw a pair of legs – my legs – emerging from it, lying completely still. There was a dark figure, very tall and thin. Its back was towards me, but I was certain it saw me. It looked like a column of rags, its tatters whipped by the wind. The water pounded the shore. The figure turned, but there was no front or back to it – it was blank on all sides. I felt something cold and empty press against me. Guillaume, a boy still, slid from the dolmen's mouth and leapt into the turf, which parted around him like water. The earth warped and surged: the green land and the grey sea and the silver sky became a ribbon of light whipping around me and I was trapped again, wedged tightly, stripping off my skin as I tore myself free.

I found myself beside my car. I had no memory of leaving the dolmen. No idea how much time had passed. The sun was sinking. My head felt like it would split open with the pain. I stood up, stumbled to the undergrowth fringing the car park and vomited. It lasted a long time, until there was nothing left but a thick bile that burned my throat. Shadows were spreading across the car park. In the next field stood a tree black with crows.

I drove through the darkness to Simrishamn, packed my things and checked out. The streets were as silent as they had been since I arrived. I drove straight to Malmö and booked into a hotel in the centre of the city. I walked the busiest streets. I ate dinner at the most crowded bar I could find. Only when it closed and I had no other choice did I go back to my hotel. In the shower the water ran grey with sand. I sat on the bed with BBC News blaring from the TV. Even with the lights on, even with the room's comforting ugly modernity all around me, I struggled to stay calm. I told myself I was exhausted. I had been anxious about presenting my paper, a paper I had worked on for months, and it had been misunderstood. I needed rest. I needed sleep.

I woke feeling wet rock pressed against my face. I heard the moan of the sea on the beach below. It grew louder. I woke again to the chatter of the TV and the room's burning brightness. I lay in bed rubbing my chest, which ached the way it had ached in France after I finally wrenched myself free. I told my mother I fell while climbing. If she knew I was lying she didn't care enough to get the truth out of me. I never spoke about it, and eventually I forgot it had ever happened.

Back in London I kept myself busy preparing my lectures, answering emails, paying bills: all tasks that bore me away from that strange episode. But the dolmen was always there, looming like a door I didn't want to open, and when my fingers found this acorn it was as if they turned the key in the lock. Now when I close my eyes I see the chamber, waiting to be filled. When I fall asleep, I feel the rock encase me. There are moments in life when we grasp what it is to die. If we're lucky we forget them, but my luck has run out.

RUN

On the long drive from Gothenburg to the farmhouse, Gunilla told David it was haunted. The owner had said so when she called to confirm the booking. 'He didn't believe it before,' she said, 'but people keep telling him things have gone missing, or been moved around with no explanation.'

'Poltergeist,' David said, doom-laden. 'Or the cleaner.' Rain crackled against the windscreen.

'He thought I'd be excited,' Gunilla said, tapping the heel of her hand against the steering wheel in time with a song on the radio. 'But who wants to share a house with someone – some*thing* – that messes with their stuff?'

'No one likes change,' David said.

'So you say. Always.'

David smiled and looked away to his right, where a long avenue of trees led to a large house painted white and yellow. Somehow it seemed to crouch on the land as if, after they had driven on, it might stand and stride away.

'Hey,' he said suddenly. 'Maybe the farm was the site of a wartime atrocity, and—'

'Enough.' Gunilla made a wall of her hand in the space between them. 'Ghosts I can take, but not more of your Nazis.'

At a rest stop they switched places. Gunilla fell asleep, and as the fields rolled past David wondered if this landscape had looked so different seventy years ago. It wasn't only because he was reading a book about Stalingrad. Being anywhere on the Continent made him think of the war. When he ate lunch in an old town square, or crossed a railway line or passed any industrial plant, he thought of Nazis. Tram systems made him think of Nazis. Bicycles made him think of Nazis. Alpine passes and quiet forests – especially quiet forests – made him think of Nazis. He could never shake his amazement that an ordinary crossroads had been a battlefield; that a park had once been stacked with bodies; that a town hall had served as headquarters for a battalion, or even a division. All these places that had been one thing had suddenly become another, and both were as real as the wheel in his hands.

When they got to the farmhouse, a long, narrow, rectangular structure screened from the road by a tall hedge and trees, David said it was so big that even if it were haunted they would never encounter its ghost. The sun was setting, and through the patio doors, a couple of miles to the east, the buildings of a neighbouring village,

Simrishamn, stood coated in red light. Beyond them, hidden from view, was the sea.

#

They had taken the house for a week. Gunilla's mother and stepfather were supposed to be there too, but the fighting had begun as soon as they arrived in Gothenburg. David had been looking forward to meeting Gunilla's family; in the year he had known her she had spoken of them so rarely and haltingly that he was delighted when she suggested the trip. But at her parents' house David spent most of the time sitting on a bench at the bottom of the garden smoking cigarettes and reading about Stalingrad. The voices of Gunilla and her mother came through the window like volleys of small-arms fire.

He only knew fragments about Gunilla. She never really knew her father; her first memory was falling into a bed of marigolds, aged two, and she had loved the smell of them ever since; expensive restaurants maddened her; stepping into a hot bath made her melancholy; wearing sunglasses, she insisted, muddied her hearing. When David asked for more she called him needy. He had never known anyone as independent as her. When she left a room it might be for five minutes, or three hours, or forever.

155

After listening to them argue for almost an hour, David went inside. He wanted to convince Gunilla to leave, but the look both women gave him made him retreat to the garden without speaking. He already knew Gunilla went for it when she fought, and now he realised where she got it from. They had argued seriously several times, but only once did he actually think it was over, that she had left him. She walked out of the flat and didn't come back for two days. When she returned she didn't say where she had been. Sitting beside her on the couch that night, eating a takeaway and drinking wine, he tried to make a joke of it: 'For a minute there I thought you weren't coming back.'

'For a minute there I wasn't,' she said, not taking her eyes off the TV.

At some point, when it had grown dark and the voices had shifted from shouting to what sounded like a quieter, more wounding intensity, Per, Gunilla's stepfather, came and sat beside David on the bench. Per spoke basic English and David knew no Swedish. David nodded and Per smiled. The windows of the house were open, and planks of yellow light ran across the lawn towards them like a bridge across a gulf.

David waved a cigarette in the direction of the house. 'Quite angry,' he said.

Per looked at the house, a half-smile on his lips and his

arms folded tightly across his broad chest. 'Not happy,' he said. They sat and listened to the shouting, and the sound of a train surging through the night. A few minutes later Per stood and stretched. He clapped his hands against his stomach. He looked at David and smiled, then shrugged. 'It has happened before,' he said. 'Tomorrow you will be gone.' He walked across the garden to the house.

#

The village where they were staying was strung along a single, gently twisting road that David thought probably used to see a handful of vehicles each day, but was now used by a steady stream of cars joining the nearby motorway. They took a walk to explore, and visited the church that stood on a low hill at one end of the village. At the perimeter of the churchyard stood a line of pollarded ash trees. They had been so severely pruned that they might have been plucked from the ground and thrust back in upside down, their shrivelled roots grasping at the air. Beyond the trees low hedges of box marked off family plots, squares of raked earth sprouting obelisks and headstones. The church walls were a dazzling white, its roof red tile. Peering through the plain panes of glass in the tall windows, David admired the spare Lutheran interior: rows of simple wooden pews faced an unadorned altar. It made

Anglican churches look showy, let alone the Catholic glitz he had known as a child.

They walked around the church and made their way to the far end of the graveyard, stopping occasionally to inspect a headstone. At the point where the graveyard ended and a field began they found a bench and a low stone table. They unpacked sandwiches and a thermos of coffee.

'It feels strange to have a picnic in a graveyard,' David said.

'In the midst of death we are in life,' said Gunilla.

David began to correct her but her look told him she meant what she had said. They drank their coffee. 'You haven't told me what you and your mum were fighting about,' David said.

Gunilla looked away over the field. She was silent for a while. 'The same things we always fight about.' She sounded very tired.

'Was it about your dad?' He had walked out when Gunilla was a toddler, and David had heard enough to work out that she blamed her mother for it. She had never heard from him again. 'It doesn't matter,' David said when Gunilla didn't respond, 'you don't have to—'

'No,' Gunilla said. 'Yes. Disagree, agree, strongly agree.' She flicked at a fly on the table, dismissing the conversation with the same gesture. David slumped back sulkily.

He told himself he didn't care. Sometimes he felt that she would let him in, that he just needed to be patient. More and more often, though, it was like this.

They walked back through the graveyard at different speeds, looking at different things. David read the names on the gravestones and tried to work out what the other words meant. The people who had died young depressed him, and the people who died old depressed him. He looked at a sand-coloured stone that marked the grave of Fredrik Gustafsson, 1918–1972. What did he do during the war? David thought. It might never have troubled his life in this backwater. But where was his family? His was the only stone in the plot, and the only name on the stone. Perhaps the rest of his family were cremated, or he had no one, and had paid for the stone himself and told the mason what to carve. David turned away and kicked at the ground.

He caught up with Gunilla at the northern corner of the graveyard, staring into a neighbouring field. The field was fallow, the grass in it several feet tall. Crows shouted overhead, and one cried out from somewhere in the grass.

'They're so loud,' David said when he was a few feet from Gunilla. She startled. 'Sorry,' he said, 'didn't mean to scare you.'

'I thought you were here already; I thought you were standing right behind me.' She looked at him, then back over her shoulder. She brushed a lock of hair behind her ear, and he saw that the skin on her arms had stippled. She laughed uncertainly and looked all around her again, but this time she was joking.

The day had grown hot. Back at the house Gunilla went inside and lay down. David tried to read his book, in which the slaughter was reaching numbing proportions, but he was too restless to concentrate. After moving to three different places around the farmhouse he gave up. He wandered through the garden and along the front of the house. The sun's brute heat persecuted him. Two large, low barns flanked the gravelly, grassy square of the farmyard, and he poked his head into one of them. The air inside was dry and tarry, the barn empty apart from some rusty, rotting tools. David walked across the yard to the other barn, where he found large sacks hanging from hooks driven into the wall. A sign, in Swedish and English, explained what should be disposed of where for recycling. He walked back outside and went around the barn. Between its blank back wall and the tall, thick hedge that screened the property from the road stood a small grove of aspens. The space within the trees was shady and cool. A gust of wind, sudden and sharp, rattled their leaves. David lay down on the grass and watched the leaves divide the sky into shifting fractions of blue. The wind strengthened, and the leaves' rattling thinned to a metallic hiss. He heard cars passing by on the other side of the hedge, waves of rushing sound that blended with the slower, more sibilant pulse of the wind. He closed his eyes and watched the sunlight flicker against his eyelids.

#

Gunilla slept the rest of the day and all through the evening. David got into bed around ten, and when he woke, just before seven, she was still lying silently beside him. He wondered if she had slept right through or had been up during the night. He showered and dressed. Eating a bowl of yoghurt and muesli on the patio, gazing at the smashed buildings on the cover of his book, he thought idly about the war.

Gunilla didn't share his interest. Each time he got another history book or novel on the subject she shook her head with what, he had come to realise, was genuine disgust. Only early on, when he tried to explain his fascination to her, had she laughed with a kind of exasperated affection. One of the few things she had told him about her family was her grandfather, remembering his childhood, saying how clean and polite the German soldiers were.

Looking across the fields, David imagined the din of tracked vehicles clanking along the lanes. In the yard behind him a group of resistance fighters were shot, their bodies buried in the aspen grove. 'Poltergeist, poltergeist,' he said quietly, 'who will avenge you?' Maybe she's right, he thought. Maybe I am childish. He closed his eyes and felt the pressure of the sun's warmth.

He started awake. The sun was higher in the sky. 'Gunilla?' he called. He looked across the open country towards Simrishamn, and at the grass-choked track leading away from the edge of the lawn. He went into the house and called her name again. His head felt heavy. How long had he been asleep? A bowl marked with white stripes of yoghurt sat in the sink. Gunilla's phone lay on the worktop.

He walked through every room and found them all empty. He beat his palms against the tops of his thighs, telling himself everything was fine. He resisted an urge to check if her clothes were still in the wardrobe. 'Gunilla!' he called into the silence.

As he stepped outside again clouds began to slip across the sun, and a line of shadow raced across the fields towards him as he saw her, coming along the track to the house. A gust of wind made the tall grass around her thrash. For a moment it seemed she was caught in a wild green sea, and a dark wave was pushing her towards him. She had a bunch of wildflowers in her hand, and was using a tree branch as a stick. When she saw him watching her she raised the stick in greeting.

'Ready for adventure?' she said as she stepped onto the patio. 'Let's get out of here.'

#

They took a long walk through the countryside and found a cafe serving a cake buffet. 'You can go back as many times as you like, you know,' Gunilla said, looking at the pastries cantilevered on David's plate.

'And I will,' he said, smiling. They sat in a sunny paved courtyard. In the flowerbeds slugs oozed across fat-leaved plants. There was a large group of older tourists sitting nearby, and a pair of hikers with a huge bronze rucksack lying at their feet, a Canadian flag pinned to it. The waitresses, all women in their fifties and sixties, wore white shirts, knee-length black skirts and dark tights. David saw the tables full of German officers drinking cognac and smoking cigarettes.

'What are you thinking about?' Gunilla asked, blowing across the surface of her coffee.

'Nothing,' David said. 'How diabetic these slugs must be.' He watched one, long and brown, mount a large cake crumb.

'Liar,' Gunilla said, her smile tight. 'You're probably thinking about soldiers. Your stupid war didn't happen here, you know.'

'Well,' David said, unable to stop himself, 'the Swedish government did allow Wehrmacht troops railway passage to and from Norway until mid '43. How do you think your grandfather got the chance to fall in love with them?'

Gunilla snorted and flicked a fragment of cake away from her. 'You are so fucking boring,' she said.

David winced. 'That's harsh,' he said. She said nothing in reply, and he decided not to either. The argument with her mum must have really got to her. He would give her some time.

In the same silence they walked down a narrow green lane to a thin strip of beach. On a rise above it stood three thatched fishermen's huts, one of which had been converted into a chapel. Running at head height around the inside of the small, low room was a ledge filled with pebbles left by visitors. On the section that ran above the rudimentary altar, children had painted images of Jesus and Mary and fishing boats on pieces of driftwood. David shut the chapel door behind him and stood alone in the quiet, dusty air. Veins of sand crossed the stone floor. The sea was a distant hiss. He had stopped believing long ago, but still found comfort in the calmness of holy spaces, especially intimate ones like this. He ran his fingers along the pebbles, some marked with names and dates: Andersson Juli 2014; Erik Parnaby; Mary and John Cartwright, England, 12/07/12. He picked up a pebble the size of his palm, smooth and pigeon-grey. He thought about what Per had said to him in Gothenburg. He replaced the pebble on the ledge and heard himself say, 'Don't let her leave.' As soon as the words left his mouth he felt ashamed. He hadn't said them. He would not remember them. He swept his hand along the shelf, the pebbles clattering to the floor.

#

That night they grilled cod and ate it on the patio with a salad, citronella candles burning in a rectangle around them. They were surrounded by an inky blackness, given depth by the distant clustered lights of Simrishamn.

'Would you get lonely living out here?' David asked.

'By myself?' said Gunilla. 'I might.'

Why by herself? he thought. 'Not with someone else?' he said.

Gunilla waved her hand, a gesture David thought might mean anything. A phone rang in the house. Their phones had the same ringtone, and both of them were inside.

'Let's leave it,' David said, 'I don't want to speak to anybody.' But Gunilla was already up. David watched her go inside, speed-walk the length of the living room and lift her phone from the kitchen counter. She raised her voice in what might have been surprise or enthusiasm. Whichever it was, it was a change from the monotone that was all he had heard since the cafe. Still talking, she moved deeper into the house. He watched her white T-shirt dwindle into the darkness of the corridor that joined the kitchen and living room to the rest of the farm-house. His meal unfinished, David threw his cutlery onto his plate and lit a cigarette. He wondered who she might be speaking to, hating that he had no idea. He thought about confronting her, but knew how foolish she would make him feel for getting angry about a phone call. Was that who he was now? Couldn't she talk to a friend on the phone? He finished his cigarette, flicked it onto the lawn and lit another. After an hour, when Gunilla still hadn't returned, he went inside and put on the TV.

#

The next morning they went for a run. They quickly left the village behind and climbed a long, low hill. At the top of the hill the road split in two. They would take one fork out, loop around and return by the other.

The day was humid, the air pressed thick between the grey sky and the dull green fields. They ran past a man in overalls inspecting a tractor. The sun broke out, then was dragged back behind the clouds. At a turn in the road stood a dead rowan, its limbs sleeved with ivy. David pointed at it.

'They plant them in graveyards at home,' he said, panting. 'They keep the dead in their graves.'

Gunilla nodded but didn't reply. She was looking at the map on her phone. She turned off the road onto a dirt path and David followed. The hot, damp air was like cotton in his mouth. They turned into the driveway of an old farmhouse, grey, half-timbered, its three sides facing a courtyard with an empty fountain. David stopped beside Gunilla. 'Is this right?' he said.

She waved her phone in a figure of eight. 'The signal,' she said.

To one side of them stood a field of green wheat. The sprouting heads of the crop gave the impression that a thin mist hung above it. In the distance stood a phalanx of wind turbines, their long blades slowly turning.

'We've gone wrong,' Gunilla said. 'This way.' She started running back the way they had come. They ran past the farmhouse again, then took a sharp right into what looked like a private garden. A dog loped towards them and they heard a woman cry out. They stopped. David bent towards the dog, a stout black Labrador, as it butted his hands. He scratched its head and neck. The woman said something in what David assumed was Swedish, but Gunilla answered in English.

'This is private property,' the woman said. The dog backed away from David and sneezed.

'Prosit,' David said automatically. He looked at the woman. She was very short, and her deeply tanned skin was tight to the bones of her face. She stood a foot shorter than Gunilla, and a foot and a half shorter than him.

'You can't run here,' she said. She spoke rapidly. She almost sounded Irish, David thought.

'We thought it was a public path,' said Gunilla.

'You can see it's my garden,' the woman said, sticking out an arm and waving it stiffly around her lawn. 'He might have attacked you. It's all right, Chilli,' she muttered to the dog, which was now lying on the ground. He panted to himself, unfazed, his back legs thrown off to one side. A scrap of wind riffled the rows of wheat standing beyond the garden.

'I'm sorry,' Gunilla said, 'I didn't know we were trespassing.' She sounded irritated. She showed the woman her phone. 'I need to get here,' she said, pointing to the road that would complete the circle of their route and take them back to the farmhouse.

The woman jabbed a finger at the end of the garden where a gap in the fence opened onto a track. 'That way,' she said, 'get going.'

Chilli pranced between them as they walked to the end of the garden, his tongue flapping from his mouth.

'Friendly lady,' David said.

'Danish bitch,' Gunilla said, wiping her forehead against her bicep.

They ran along an uneven track dividing two large fields of green wheat. David looked across the fields at the turbines in the distance. He imagined he could hear their great blades slicing the air, a menacing, monumental sound. He wanted to talk to Gunilla but he couldn't think of anything she'd want to hear. They were running at different speeds, now one catching up, now the other pulling ahead.

They rejoined the road, which ran between more wheat fields. The fields were green to the left and a dirty gold to the right. Small clouds passed across the sun, pools of shadow lying on the wheat. David ran past two thick black skid marks that ran on for fifty feet, reaching their darkest point then suddenly stopping. He wondered what the driver had been trying to avoid, and if they had succeeded.

Some distance had opened between them, and David widened it still further. He made his tired legs move faster. At the end of his burst he stopped, his breath scorching his chest. He bent over, hands on his knees, and sucked in air. He spat. Blood throbbed in his temples and crowded his vision, making the tarmac at his feet crawl. He spat again.

As his vision cleared he heard an intricate piping fill the air around him, long lines of melody tumbling from the sky. Standing up straight, hands on hips, still breathing hard, he saw a skylark hovering above him. The bird alternately beat its wings and stilled them, its rushing music continuing without pause. Then it suddenly plummeted down towards the ground – like a Stuka, David thought – and flew away, rising rapidly from the land.

He looked across the fields. The wind blew and the wheat was pushed down and to the side as if hands were searching through it. He turned around, expecting Gunilla to be approaching, but he saw her still distant, standing in the middle of the road. He waved but she didn't respond, only stared in his direction. A small black car rounded the corner behind her and slowed to a stop. She turned and leaned on the off-side door. She spoke, but she was too far away for David to hear what she was saying. The sun's glare filled the windscreen, stopping him from seeing who was inside.

He knew exactly what was going to happen next. He moved a small, useless step towards Gunilla as she straightened, opened the car door and got in. The car reversed, neatly and at speed, turned a tight semicircle and drove away. David started to run and stopped. He ran again and stopped again. The car took a corner and disappeared from view, the noise of its engine growing fainter and fainter until it could no longer be heard. He waited for it to turn around and come back. The sun had been quenched and the wind had died. In the distance stood the turbines, their blades still.

David ran into the driveway expecting to see the car there; he expected Gunilla and her mystery friend to be waiting with beers and explanations: a big joke. But there was no car, and inside the house there was no one. His phone was on the kitchen counter. He picked it up and called her. It went straight to voicemail. At the sound of her recorded voice a cramp of panic gripped his belly. He went into their bedroom and saw her things were gone. Maybe there was a ghost after all, he thought. It took her things. It took her.

He walked back out of the house and stood in the yard, his hands on top of his head. He stared into the grey sky. The wind stirred. He walked past the empty barns to the aspen grove. The wind blew through the trees and their leaves hissed like the ocean. Their limbs creaked. Traffic rushed past on the other side of the hedge. He lay on the cool grass. The tree branches weaved like hands above him. Tomorrow he would be gone, leaving no trace. He listened to the cars drive by, each one refusing to slow and turn.

PORTALS

I went to Paris to meet a girl called Monica. I've never forgotten it. She was a dancer from Spain. I met her at a wedding in Barcelona where the groom was the only person I knew. We really got on, Monica and me and her boyfriend Victor. We drank a lot and told stories, and Victor and me took it in turns dancing with Monica.

We added each other on Facebook but didn't really stay in touch. Then, a year after the wedding, Monica messaged me to say she was going to visit a friend in Paris. She wasn't with Victor any more, she said, and she wanted to see me. *I really liked spending time with you at the wedding*, she wrote. I bought a Eurostar ticket the same day.

That first night we took it easy and went for dinner at a place beside the Seine. You couldn't see the river from the restaurant, though, only the stone balustrade that ran above it, a thick band of mauve sky and a stream of cars. There was Monica, me, Tanis, the childhood friend Monica was visiting, and Tanis's French boyfriend Alex, who was a bit of an arsehole. She was a real talker, and he was always shutting her down.

– Tanis, he'd say, making it sound like 'tennis' – Tanis, don't exhaust our guest. He has only just arrived in our city.

Or – Tanis, Tanis, don't be so . . . *Iberian*, looking at me like he was Oscar fucking Wilde.

But I didn't say anything to him. After all, I didn't really know any of these people.

– Is Alex always such a dick? I asked Monica as we walked beside the river. Tanis and Alex were a little way ahead of us.

She covered her face with her hands and groaned. – Yes! Always! I love Tanis so much but her boyfriends are . . . are shit. You can't tell her, though. You try and it's— she put her fingers in her ears and shook her head. We stopped, waiting for a gap in the traffic. Tanis and Alex were already on the other side of the street.

– Where have all the good men gone, Stephen? Monica said, looking up at me, her large green eyes framed by curls of glossy black hair. She said it like she was quoting it from somewhere, like I was supposed to know the next line.

– When I find out I'll let you know, I said, immediately wishing I'd said something else. I wasn't smart enough to know that I could have said anything. That at this point the actual words we said to each other didn't really matter at all.

#

The next morning I ate breakfast in the sad little restaurant at my hotel, where everyone else was dressed for business meetings, then went to meet Monica. We took the metro north, to the flea market at Clignancourt. Tanis had told us about it at dinner. – It's like *Blade Runner*! she said, – or Thunderdome!

Walking from the metro we crossed the concrete trench of the Périphérique, a torrent of cars rushing beneath us. On the far side of the bridge the market began: haphazard stalls selling handbags, and tall racks of shiny leather coats overlapping each other like scales. Traders were selling phone covers and cuddly toys, fake luggage, baseball caps, basketball shirts, trainers, sunglasses and phone cards. Hip-hop and Arabic pop blared from speakers hooked to the awnings of the stalls, and the air was greasy with burning oil from falafel stands.

We came to a gate in a wall. Passing through it was like teleporting: we left all the chaos and noise behind and walked down narrow lanes with ivy growing across the walls. – It's like Provence, – Monica said. Here the traders didn't have stalls, but snug garage-like spaces. Most of them were selling antiques, and a jumble of furniture spilled onto the narrow pavements: metal garden chairs, school desks, benches and scarred kitchen tables. Monica stopped beside a chaise longue with a group of porcelain rabbits scattered across it, turning the white fabric beneath them into a snowfield. Beside it a man sat slumped in a battered leather armchair, reading a paper. A knotted trunk ran up the wall behind him, disappearing into a mass of triangular green leaves. Long tendrils weaved out from the leaves like serpents.

– What kind of tree is that? I asked Monica. The owner lowered his paper, studied us for a moment and went back to the news.

– In Spanish it's glicinas, she said.

– Glee-thee-nass, I repeated.

– Yes, glicinas.

– C'est 'glycine' en français, the man said, lowering his paper for a second time and pausing dramatically. – Not for sale.

We took the metro back into the city. We got off at Les Halles and walked through the cobblestone streets of the Marais, past tiny art galleries and expensive clothes shops. We had settled into each other's rhythm, it felt like, and we were touching each other more and more – my hand on her shoulder, hers in the small of my back or on my arm as she pointed something out. It was a comfortable feeling.

We ended up lying on a patch of grass on a peaceful square surrounded by old stone arcades. Monica's face was so close to mine that I could feel her breath. Nearby a girl sat cross-legged, sawing at her violin. The way it scraped and squeaked was a disaster, but the look on her face, intense and earnest, suggested it was meant to sound that way.

Monica told me about the next piece her company was doing, something abstract with guns. – Guns are sexy, she said. – It's corny to say it, maybe, but it's true. Everyone says America, America, crazy with guns. But look at the stories we watch all the time. All guns. We love the drama of a gun.

– But sexy? Really?

– Of course! Have you fired one?

– I haven't.

– I have. It feels totally sexy. She laughed. – I sound so fascist! She was wearing these wide-legged black trousers, and as she spoke she raised and lowered her right leg in stages: just above the ground, at forty-five degrees, at ninety, and as her leg rose her trouser leg dropped and gathered at her knee. I watched her calf muscle tense and slacken and tense again as she rotated her foot.

– You're not a fascist, I said.

– What a sweet thing to say, she said, and laughed again.

I looked into her eyes' bright green. It put me on edge, the way they shone. I rolled onto my back and looked at the milk-white sky. I reached for her hand. It was sweaty.

A little boy and girl ran around us laughing, each one chasing the other. I closed my eyes. Listening to them, and to the girl's violin braying like a dying animal, I fell asleep.

I must have only slept for a minute. When I opened my eyes Monica was sleeping too. Her hand was still in mine. I studied the crumbs of mascara in her eyelashes, the tiny creases in her lips. She had these incredible swollen lips. When her eyes opened I rolled onto my back and fake-yawned, pretending I'd just woken up.

– We should go, I said, releasing her hand.

– Why?

I turned and looked at her. Staring at me she shifted her body, rolling onto her back. It was an invitation, but I hesitated. This was exactly what I had come for, but now the tiny space between us felt unbridgeable. To be there again! I was in front of a door I'd been searching for, only now I couldn't reach out and turn the handle.

– We should head back, I said. We were going to a party that night. We picked ourselves up and brushed curls of dead grass off our clothes. Monica was silent as we walked to the metro. When I said I might walk all the way back to my hotel she only shrugged. – See you in a few hours then, I said when we reached the entrance.

She just nodded and held her fingers up in the shape of a phone. – I'll call you, she said without turning around, descending the stairway into the tunnels.

\#

After I showered I lay on the bed, smoked a cigarette and watched the news. A plane had gone down in the Mediterranean: a striped tailfin floated in open water, with smaller debris scattered around it. The footage, shot from a helicopter, showed several small boats circling the wreckage. The report cut to weeping relatives at an airport. The chances were nearly zero, but it had happened to them. And some lucky fucker overslept and missed the flight. I turned the TV off. Thinking about Monica, a thrill of anticipation snaked through me. I'd blown it that afternoon, but next time I wouldn't hesitate.

\#

We were going to a house party in the nineteenth, but first we had drinks at an apartment across the street from the Buttes-Chaumont Park. The apartment was on the fifth floor of an old building with no lift. The lights in the stairwell were set on timers so stingy we couldn't even make it up one flight before they went out, leaving us to grope our way towards the next orange dot. Camille, a French girl who worked with Tanis, lived in the apartment with two guys, Michel and Alain. Loud house music was playing, and Camille and Alain were making jugs of vodka cocktails. Everyone was smoking, and even with the two long, narrow windows open to the night the room – a cramped kitchen–living room – was foggy with it.

It was obvious by the way Michel talked to Monica that he wanted her. He tried to act like I didn't exist. We had been talking in English – I had apologised for not being able to speak his language – but then he asked Monica something in French anyway.

– Oui, Monica said and then turned to me. – Michel asked if I'm a dancer. Remember, she said to Michel, – Stephen doesn't speak French.

– Of course! Michel said, inclining his head towards me. – We will all speak his language, then. He turned back to Monica. – You dancers have to look after your bodies very well, he said, looking her up and down.

– Oh yes, very much, Monica laughed, shaking her drink and cigarette as counter-evidence. – Do you guys exercise? she said. – You're both in good shape.

– Bicycle, Michel answered quickly. – I cycle everywhere. And swim. A few times a week.

You could see it. He had a good body. In my case – no muscle, skinny – Monica was just being polite.

– Tell me more about your dancing, Michel said, leaning his face closer to Monica's. – I love dance.

I poured myself a drink, lit another cigarette and imagined shoving Michel out of the window.

As we descended to the street our voices echoed in the stairwell. On each flight the darkness would swallow us for a couple of seconds until Camille or Alain, leading the way, hit the next switch. In front of me Monica and Tanis were deep in conversation. About halfway down, as the darkness struck again, a hand held my face and someone pressed their lips to mine. When the light came on Monica was there, smiling at me. She turned and ran ahead to catch up with Tanis.

#

It was a warm night, and the courtyard belonging to the flat, a well-like space between tall apartment buildings, was crammed with people. No one had said anything about fancy dress, but a lot of people had come as movie characters and historical figures. A Marcel Marceau, with a white face and a trail of black tears inked down one cheek, looked me up and down and said something in French.

– Anglais? I said.

– You didn't want to wear a costume?

– I didn't know I was supposed to.

He looked sad about it, but then he looked sad about everything.

I lost track of Camille and Alain; and, happily, of Michel. Monica, Tanis and I moved inside and established ourselves in a corner of the kitchen. We had bought vodka on the way, and on the cluttered counter we found cups and a bottle of tonic, and a bag of ice standing in its own meltwater. I'd had a few drinks by then and was well on the way, which is why I told Tanis she deserved better than Alex, that he was a bully and a bore. She looked confused for a moment, then angry.

– He's . . . it's not as simple as that, she said. Monica said something in Spanish that sounded soothing and Tanis shrugged, still looking pissed off, and reached for the vodka bottle. Monica looked at me and pointed towards the living room, packed with dancers.

– When will we dance? she said.

– I can't dance with a professional.

– You danced with me in Barcelona, she said. – And this 'professional', she wagged her fingers around the word, – is drunk.

I went to the toilet and when I came back they were talking to someone called Guy. He was English, living in Paris doing some modelling and what he called 'odds and sods'. He was excited about going to see some DJ. He said we should come along and I said sure, but Monica and Tanis said they couldn't.

– Come on, I said, grabbing Monica at the waist. – We'll dance, just like you wanted.

– No, she said, smiling, swaying a little with her hands

on my forearms. – We need to wait for Alex. We can dance here.

– I don't like the music here. Tell Alex to meet us at the club.

– He doesn't like clubs, Tanis said.

I was fired up to go. I wanted to swap this house and all this talking for the noise and dark of a club. – Forget about Alex, I said. He can go fuck himself, I thought.

Tanis and Monica had an exchange in Spanish. Tanis repeated a two-word phrase several times, sounding tenser with each repetition. – OK, Monica said. She turned to me. – We promised we would meet him here. We are going to wait. Will you wait with us?

– Where's the club? I asked Guy. I had him repeat the address to Tanis, who put it in her phone. I could tell Monica was surprised I was leaving, but she didn't say anything. I got a thrill from upsetting her. It's ridiculous to me now, but I was furious she was putting that tosser Alex ahead of me. I told her if I didn't see her at the club I'd call her in the morning, that we'd have breakfast. I held up my fingers in the shape of a phone and walked away.

#

– Is that your girlfriend? Guy asked me as we got out onto the street.

– No, I said. – A friend.

– She's really fit.

Hearing that I wanted to tell Guy she *was* my girl-friend, and that we were in love. – She's a dancer, was all I said. – She's great.

The further we got from the party the better I felt. We were both drunk, and neither of us wanted to shut up. We talked about festivals, clubs we liked, drugs we'd taken. The streets seemed quiet for Saturday night, although I guess it was Sunday morning by then. It was a long walk, but we never discussed getting a cab or finding a train. We went through a tunnel, and past a factory, and down a cob-bled street that was mysteriously wet – it hadn't rained all day, but the cobbles glistened like oil. We walked down a street of mechanics' workshops, their metal shutters busy with graffiti. We went through a gate into a small court-yard, then passed through a low doorway with a bouncer posted beside it. The club was a single long room: hot, loud and heaving with people. The walls were beaded with moisture. The music was drum and bass: staccato beats riveting the air, and bass so powerful it made the building shudder in long blurs of vibration. The humid air ran across my face like fingertips. On top of all the drink Guy had given me a pill. Dexamphetamine, he said. It wasn't so strong but I could definitely feel it; I was gulp-ing my beer and chain-smoking cigarettes.

We danced for a long time. It might have been a couple of hours later that I saw Monica and Tanis squeezing their way across the packed dancefloor. Behind them
came Alex, looking miserable, then Michel. Monica saw
me and thrust her chin up in acknowledgement, but she
didn't smile and she stopped with some distance still between us. She was already dancing, her body flowing. It
was incredible to watch her; she didn't hit the beats but
wove herself between them. A harsh melody came strafing
across the breakbeat and her body warped in response, as
if an invisible force was shaking her. Her back arched, her
hands joined one another, and her arms twisted an orbit
up around her torso and over her head. I saw Michel behind her, his hands moving to her hips. I stopped dancing
and stood there, jostled by the people around me. Monica moved her body against Michel. Her hand went to
his neck and held it, held it with what seemed to me at
the time, on drugs and fifteen feet away in a dark and
crowded room, like infinite tenderness. I started pushing
my way through the crowd. I wanted to stand in front of
them; I wanted to see the shame on Monica's face. Tanis
waved but I ignored her. Michel was whispering something in Monica's ear. I reached out and placed my hand
on his shoulder. He shrugged it off. I pulled my arm back,
made a fist and drove it into his face. I haven't been in
many fights, but every other one has been scrappy and

indecisive. This, though, was the cleanest hit: Michel went down so fast it was like I made him disappear. A space cleared around us. Monica – who I never saw or spoke to again – looked at me like she didn't even know me. Which she didn't, I realised. I laughed. It was so ridiculous and sad.

– Time to go, said Guy, pulling my arm. I saw two bouncers ploughing across the dancefloor towards us. We got to the entrance and he pushed me out into the coolness of the early morning, past the doorman, who glanced up from his phone at me. I ran, and when I couldn't run any more I walked, and kept walking. I felt exhilarated, but I was wiping tears from my eyes. I had been challenged, and I'd met the challenge, but what was I doing now? I should have been in my hotel room with Monica, not walking these pale, empty streets. If I could go back and talk to that person I'd tell him to open every door you come to while you've got the chance; there aren't as many as you think. The sky was purple. I was shaky with tiredness and adrenaline and the end of the drugs, but it was good to be walking. I wanted to walk forever. My hand burned like it was aflame. When the sun broke through, the streets became golden rivers.

JOHNNY KINGDOM

'I shouldn't joke,' Andy says, 'my doctor told me I'm dying. "I want a second opinion," I said. "OK," he says, "you're ugly."' Andy presses a handkerchief to his face and shakes his head in despair. 'My luck,' he says, 'Jesus. I was making love to this girl and she started crying. I say, "Should I stop?" She says, "You've started?"' Andy talks, the audience laughs. Superstition dictates that he always begin with the exact same line; the act will collapse if he doesn't. It's not Kingdom's funniest bit, but it's his favourite: short, absurd, and drenched in sexual failure. 'I was with this girl. She loved me so much. "You're like nothing else, Johnny. You get me so hot, Johnny." She was the girl of my dreams.' A shrug. 'But then I woke up.' He clenches the tie. Rotates the shoulder. Hits them again.

The older crowd like the 'I was so ugly' stuff: 'Talk about ugly. When I was born the doctor slapped my mother.' The bachelor parties like wife jokes. His wife, Sylvia, hates the bachelor parties. 'Kegs and strippers and all that . . . *spurting* testosterone,' she says, wrinkling her nose and giving her head a slow, sad shake. 'A hundred kinds of ugly.' She takes his chin in a loose grip and fixes her eyes on his. 'You keep your nose clean, buster.'

#

'During sex my wife's a screamer. Last night I had to go next door to complain.' Andy is in front of around thirty people in Syracuse, New York, a four-hour drive from home. The joke, like all of Andy's jokes, is Johnny Kingdom's. So are his movements and mannerisms. 'People treat me like dirt,' he mutters, microphone held tight to his chest as he dabs a crushed handkerchief against his sodden face. His body is a perpetual shrug of anxiety: restless steps backwards and forwards, shoulder rolls, an obsessive-compulsive reaching for the tie knot. Kingdom's stage persona was a train wreck: a horny, inept loser with a cheating wife, hateful kids and chronic bad luck. His jokes have always made Andy laugh, even the really stupid ones.

In a small backstage office smelling of old beer, Andy collects his money. 'Glad to have you,' the manager says. 'Never thought I'd see Johnny Kingdom playing Jesters.'

'You didn't,' Andy says.

#

Andy doesn't like any of the names for what he does. He rejects 'impersonator', and resists 'tribute act', although he knows it comes closest. But the website he takes his bookings through, and the posters he puts up on bulletin boards at community centres, colleges and retirement homes, can't afford to be coy: *Johnny Kingdom Performs LIVE for YOU! Andy Tower IS Johnny Kingdom: A Fraction of the Talent at a Fraction of the Price!*

Andy makes himself up to look like Kingdom, does his bits, and takes his laughs and his applause. To his continuing surprise, the bookings keep coming in. He doesn't make nearly enough to cover the family expenses – they get by on what Sylvia makes – but at least this way he can contribute something. The Kingdom thing is supposed to be giving him time to work on his own material, but he's stuck. Blocked. Sometimes, although less and less frequently these days, Sylvia asks him how it's going, and he says, 'Fine,' and changes the subject. Kingdom was old before he made it. His career misfired and he spent a decade selling aluminium siding to support his wife and kids. He was nowhere, but he came back at age forty, Andy's age, in the face of everyone telling him to give it up. Andy knows he's stuck, but he still thinks – those times when he can face thinking about it at all – that something will come. Things will turn around. Then he'll send Kingdom away for ever.

Andy is in the kitchen buttering toast. Sylvia walks in and asks him to drive her to the optometrist. She's out of contacts, and doesn't like driving in her glasses because they slide down her nose. One day when she's pushing them back up, she says, she'll crash the car and die, 'and then where will you and the boys be?'

'Barbados?'

She doesn't laugh.

'We used to laugh more,' he says.

'You were funny when we met,' she deadpans, a little too well.

'You were shitfaced when we met,' he says, and now, to his relief, she does laugh.

He came to America for what he thought was a holiday. Back in London he started the way most people did: open mics in pub function rooms, or sweating basements, the rooms always too hot or too cold, and usually too empty. But his favourite comics had always been American: Allen, Wright, Hedberg, but before them all came Kingdom, ever since a friend gave him a taped copy of *Deadbeat* when he was fourteen years old. So when he came to the States it was as a kind of pilgrimage. Within a week he met Sylvia, at a tiny comedy club in Brooklyn, and started talking as soon as he saw her. Back then he was confident and ambitious in a way he finds difficult to grasp now: it propelled him almost without his having to think about it. It wasn't even that his material was so good; all that seemed to matter was his belief in it. Talking to Sylvia in that club had been the same: he wanted to do it, so he did it. Success was lying around him in chunks that he just had to reach down and pick up. When he thinks back, it feels more like something from a book or a film than part of his own life. It had never been so simple again. What scares him is that if today's Andy were in that same club, sitting at that same sticky bar, he wouldn't even be able to speak to Sylvia, and if he did, she would look right through him like he didn't exist.

#

Before shows Andy takes a few moments alone in his dressing room, which is almost never a dressing room. Usually it's an administrator's cramped office with a family portrait on the desk and framed certificates on the wall, or a storage room, or, if it's a bachelor party, a bedroom, or even just his car. The paint stick he uses is melanoma orange and takes days to come off entirely; towels come away from his body marked with faecal stains. 'Turin shrouds,' Sylvia calls them. She will appear in the doorway, a dirty towel stretched above her head, crying, 'The

Messiah! The Messiah!' This was a joke between them once, but it has become something else. They have always had ups and downs, but lately Andy has detected a sourness that wasn't there before. He knows they have a lot to talk about, but not talking about it is so much easier. Better to talk about what the kids are up to, or groceries, or to make a joke; or sometimes to just not talk at all.

Getting into costume is a ritual for Andy. He thinks of it as a gate in the wall that divides him from his onstage persona. Peering into his compact mirror, he silently runs through jokes he can tell backwards. Fate has given him a nose not as uncommonly broad as Kingdom's, but large enough to work as homage. Everything else is wardrobe. He puts on his wig cap, its scratchy net making him feel like his forehead has a low current running through it. He uses spirit gum to fix a fake mole the size of a pencil eraser to his right cheek, near the nostril. He puts on a scarlet tie and black suit jacket. For a bachelor party or college booking he hams things up: a powder-blue shirt so frilled it looks like it once flurried along the ocean floor, and a plum-coloured velvet jacket he found at a Goodwill.

The Kingdom act had been intended as a one-off when he tried it eight years before. He had worked his most recent half hour till it was threadbare, and the lack of good new material was starting to feel like a drought.

He enjoyed the feeling of laughs – laughs he was finding so difficult to win with his own lines – dropping into his hand like fruit from a tree. So he did it one more time, then another time after that. He started getting on the bottom of bills at serious venues on the east coast, places he hadn't been close to cracking before: Comedy Connection in Boston; Gotham in New York; even Carolines one time, where Hedberg himself had done his last ever show. He hadn't expected it, and he couldn't explain it – Kingdom was dead, and about as unfashionable as you could get – but the rooms responded.

Not that the response was always positive, and it was rarely unanimous. People had trouble getting the act. Were they supposed to be laughing *with* Andy or *at* him? Was it tribute? Was it mockery? The uncertainty appealed to some bookers, but the real bottom line was that people came and they bought booze, which is the only thing that matters to a comedy club. And there was a kind of timelessness to the material, Andy thought. Kingdom's arsenal of one-liners was infinitely adaptable, and he didn't think it made a lot of difference if people thought a mother-in-law joke was being told straight or ironic, as long as they laughed.

There was only one thing other comics liked about the act: when you go on after someone strange, you get another angle to work. The audience will reward you just for not confusing them. It's all part of the show. The MC would walk on as Andy walked off, and right after the handshake would throw the crowd a bamboozled look and point a thumb at Andy's disappearing back as if to say, 'What's with that guy?' The laugh that got, Andy felt, really belonged to him. The only one in the whole set that did.

Andy didn't have any illusions about other comics' opinions of what he was doing – he was ashamed of it himself – but he made himself stay and hang out after shows rather than sloping off like he wanted to. Face to face they often didn't know how to take him, and when they found out he was English too, well, what the fuck was that about? He explained this was a temporary thing; that he was working on his own material; that none of this was planned. Sometimes there was aggression, and he could understand that. Sometimes he was asked, with genuine puzzlement, why he was doing someone else's bits – a crime in comedy, but complicated in his case by the fact that he wasn't trying to pass someone else's line off as his own, he was openly performing someone's entire act. Of course Kingdom had bought in jokes by the yard, lots of comics used writers, and why couldn't you cover jokes like you can cover a song? But he never made the argument because he basically agreed with the objections. He was as uncomfortable with what he was doing as anyone else was.

Despite that, Andy couldn't always stand there and take it if someone told him what he was doing was bullshit – which he knew every single one of them was thinking, whether they broadcast it or not. He tried to ignore it, but one night in Philadelphia he couldn't hold back. He had opened for Marvin Butler, a skinny mock-hipster with bubble perm and outsized glasses whose set he watched and enjoyed. But backstage after the show, Butler called Andy a necrophiliac. 'Yeah? Well you'd better watch out then, Marvin,' Andy said in Kingdom's voice, grabbing two hips of air and thrusting his groin furiously towards them, 'because when I look at you I see a fucking dead man.'

As the act gathered momentum, Andy's agent – when he still had an agent – urged him to prepare a plan B in case Kingdom's estate took any notice and tried to shut him down. Or if people simply lost interest, as sooner or later they would, because sooner or later they always did. Andy assured him he had routines of his own ready to go, but that wasn't true. Nothing would come. All he had were scraps. But as it turned out, scraps were all it took: he started trying to smuggle his lines in between Kingdom's, and everything went wrong. The shifts in tone were bewildering; the change threw his delivery off; his own material just wasn't funny enough. He lost count of the times he died, losing one room after another. He could only fight the silences with Kingdom's help, the last person's help he wanted. And even then, there was only so much Johnny could do.

#

On weekday mornings they eat breakfast very early, as a family, so Sylvia can see Tim and Marcus before her commute to the city. It is barely light outside and the spotlights above the table are on. Sylvia feeds Marcus while Tim quietly spoons cereal into his mouth. Tim is habitually withdrawn – Asperger's was suspected at one point, but they had him tested and he isn't on the spectrum. Apparently this is just the way he is. 'I'm not surprised,' Andy said at the time. 'I was a lot like him when I was a kid.'

'That's not reassuring,' Sylvia had said. 'At all.'

'So I have some news,' Andy says, tapping a knife against his glass of orange juice. Sylvia looks at him expectantly. Marcus stares at the yoghurt in the spoon she's holding. Tim's rhythm of spoon to bowl to mouth continues unchanged. 'This next bachelor party? The one in Florida? That is it. No more after that.'

Sylvia smiles. 'Really?' she says. 'But why? I mean, don't those things keep you on your toes?'

He's told her that before, and it's true, working those

drunk, boisterous crowds does keep certain muscles strong, but he wants to do something for her. He feels like he hasn't in so long. At the same time, he's worried about her reaction if he tells her that, so he has planned what to say. 'I've had a breakthrough, with my writing. I mean this could be *really* good, so I need more time to work on it.'

'You're writing again, Andy,' is all she says, and for a moment he shares the simple joy of her statement before remembering there has been no breakthrough; that there is no writing.

He forces himself to shrug and smile. 'We'll see where it goes,' he says.

'It's going to be great,' Sylvia says, guiding a spoonful of yoghurt into Marcus's mouth. 'And *you*, little man,' she says, the boy's eyes widening as she addresses him, 'should be doing this yourself. Right, Dad?'

Marcus squirms in his seat and looks at Andy.

'You want to know what I think, Marcus?' Andy says.

Marcus nods.

Andy mashes his spoon into his forehead and lumps of yoghurt and muesli fall down his face. Even Tim smiles.

'My husband the comic genius,' says Sylvia.

\#

Andy has two gigs in Florida: the bachelor party that only he is calling his farewell show, and, the night before, one of his regular retirement village bookings. Suzzy, social co-ordinator at Sawgrass Meadow, is there to meet him at Tampa. 'Suzzy like fuzzy!' she told him when they first met, a few years ago. Suzzy is skinny, spry and tanned to the colour and texture of one of Andy's longest-serving towels. He has never known anyone as enthusiastic as Suzzy. When she grins, which is often, she throws her entire upper body into it. As he comes through the gate, in a foul mood he sank into as his plane laboured into the dirty New Jersey sky, he sees her hopping on the spot and waving, holding aloft a handwritten sign like she always does and that he wishes she would not. It says JOHNNY K.

'How's Sylvia?' Suzzy asks once they're on the freeway. Her little Toyota is so pungent with pine freshener Andy thinks he can feel his skin burning.

'She's good,' Andy says. 'Working too hard, but she's good.'

'And the little ones? Getting not-so-little now, I'll bet.'

'That's right,' Andy says. 'Tim's got gigantism, so we can't even have him in the house any more. He sleeps in the woodshed.'

'Is that a joke?' Suzzy says, her smile faltering.

'I never joke,' Andy says, staring at the road with the sullenness of a teenager.

Suzzy is silent for a moment, then carries on with the catch-up as if nothing has happened. 'Your youngest is Marcus, right? Is he four now?'

'Marcus *is* four. You have an incredible memory, Suzzy,' Andy says, impressed despite himself. He sees her just twice a year, but she seems to remember everything he has ever told her about his family.

'Four!' Suzzy says. 'That's a magical age.'

'It is,' Andy says, although he doesn't agree. What Marcus mostly does is run at things until either he falls over or they do. Fun, but hardly magical. Although at least dealing with him is straightforward, unlike solemn Tim. Sometimes when Andy rehearses the act Tim stares at him like he's reciting a list of war dead. Andy breaks off and asks him, 'Any good?'

'Very good,' Tim says, like a put-upon butler. Andy has watched him play with his action figures, his soldiers and superheroes, which don't yell at each other and fight, but sigh and walk away. He finds them in random corners of the house, manipulated into poses of lonely contemplation. Arriving at classmates' birthday parties, Andy has seen him methodically shake everyone's hand, like a funeral director offering condolences.

'Speaking of four, Mr Kingdom,' Suzzy says with mischief, 'did you know it's four years since you first came to Sawgrass?'

'Is that right?' says Andy. He knows it is. A gloomy anniversary mocked by an immaculate Tampa sky. He wants to punch the glove compartment. Suzzy is talking but he doesn't listen to her. He remembers how difficult things were between him and Sylvia the first time he came down here. She had been enormous, two weeks from her due date, and when the booking came in he said he wasn't taking it. He expected her to be happy, but she said they couldn't afford to turn down the money. When he said screw the money she told him the truth was she could do with the time alone. She went into labour when he was flying back – he picked up a voicemail when he landed – and by the time he got to the hospital Marcus was there, tiny and all-powerful. Sylvia's sister had been her birth partner instead of him, and ever since he had pretended he was OK with that.

'. . . and we always sell a mountain of tickets as soon as your poster goes up,' Suzzy is saying. 'You're a bona fide Sawgrass favourite.'

Andy's gigs down here are almost always sold out, and while he tells himself this is because of the audience's lack of alternatives at places like this – 'twilight facilities,' Sylvia calls them, and my god does he love her mind – he has to allow that, on this sclerotic circuit at least, he really is a hit.

Suzzy drops Andy off at the same guest bungalow he

is always given. He thinks it is, anyway: everything looks the same here. The bungalow's slat boards are brilliantly white, its compact interior pristine. All down the silent street the identical white houses glow like phosphor in the sun.

'Pick you up at six,' Suzzy calls from the open window, pulling away from a verge so vividly green it looks like it's moving. Later on she will drive him to the administrators' cafeteria for dinner and take him to his dressing room, which is her office. He will admire photographs of her grandchildren, whose names he never even tries to remember: 'This one looks well'; 'What a lovely smile she has'; 'That one really gets around!' He will perform in the function room of the Sawgrass Country Club, a venue whose name evokes dark wood and polished brass, but the reality of which is beige walls and stain-obscuring patterned carpets.

After the show Suzzy will drive him back to his bungalow, where he'll watch TV until he falls asleep. His first time here, his post-show adrenaline blended with anger at and concern for Sylvia, he tried walking back in an effort to tire himself out. Eventually, though, hopelessly lost, he had to call Suzzy to rescue him from the labyrinth of marshmallow houses that ran on and on in every direction. Even the shrubs in their soil borders were uniform. She arrived in a lemon-yellow dressing gown and

Birkenstocks, her face covered in a thick, green cream. She was radiating energy. Andy wondered if she really slept, or just wore different clothes at night to reassure people.

As soon as he starts his set, he knows it will be one of those rare ones where everything glides frictionlessly into place. His timing is as good as it has ever been, his intonation flawless. He resists the temptation he feels, when a show is going well, to slip in some of his own bits. And if he ignores the fact that this material is the last thing he wants to be doing, if he views the gig as a purely technical exercise, as opposed to a creative one, then it really is close to perfect. 'Boy, what a hotel that was,' he says, mopping his face with his handkerchief, 'that bedsheet could've been exhibit A in a homicide and two paternity suits.' He waits, and just as the laughter begins to recede says, 'But Christ, I was an ugly kid' – and already there is laughter, anticipatory, because they trust him now. 'So ugly,' he says, shaking his head. 'Anytime I got lost my parents just followed the screams.'

It sweeps up and rushes over him again, all the barks and croaks and smokers' rasps. A wave of joy. Most of these people have probably seen him before, he thinks. How many times have they heard these jokes? Here, on TV, on records. And how many times has he told them? He feels powerful and miserable, and like laughing himself.

'What a crowd, what a crowd,' he mumbles. He steps forwards, backwards. He waggles his tie like a key in a stiff lock. 'And pimples? Oh boy. When a blind guy touched my face he said, "Braille!" You know what he told me it said? "Don't look!"'

The laughter has taken on its own momentum. It has grown so strong and then helpless that all he needs to do for the next few moments is prod it with a look or a shrug, or a double take at some imagined offstage mis-behaviour. 'Yeah,' he says absently, staring into the space above the audience as he straightens his tie and stretch-es his neck. He jerks onto tiptoes and looks behind him, as if goosed by an invisible hand. He does all this with-out thinking about it, kneading the laughter like dough. He can hear people hiccoughing, crying, sucking in air like they're suffocating. Women hand each other Klee-nexes. Men blow their noses into handkerchiefs big as sails pulled from blazer pockets. Nothing's sadder than a roomful of laughing people. Andy can't remember whose that is. Maybe it's his.

After that kind of show, even at a place like Sawgrass Meadow, the adrenaline kick is hefty, and Andy knows he won't be sleeping for a few hours. Declining Suzzy's offer of a lift but armed with directions, he leaves the venue and is enfolded by the humid Tampa night. Suzzy's spidery handwriting tells him he needs to turn left onto Vivien

Leigh, then look for Larry Hagman a couple of blocks up on the right. The naming convention has changed since he was here last because, Suzzy explained, it wasn't just Andy 'that one time you slipped my leash' who had trouble finding the way home. Streets that had formerly been vanilla forgettable – Mimosa Drive, Magnolia Way – now bore the names of era-appropriate actors, 'because even when someone doesn't recognise their own husband, they still remember Cary Grant. Oh, and before you ask,' she added, powering up that devastating grin, 'there's no Johnny Kingdom. Yet.'

He walks past the identical bungalows. Already, precise memories of tonight's show are fading, his sense of achievement dwindling. His triumph degrades into an edgy energy. Walking along Richard Chamberlain, his thoughts skitter between bits of his routine, concern for Tim – always there somewhere, like a radio playing in another room – and anger with himself for that stupid lie he told Sylvia about writing again. He cycles through the projects he has abandoned over the last few years, something he has done with decreasing regularity since the last time he actually began something new. Turning onto James Stewart he decides none of them are salvageable. It's time to trash them all and start fresh. Or maybe just do the first part, and find some other way to fill his time. He sees a dim shape – a possum? – shambling across a lawn. He yawns. Barbra Streisand, Burt Reynolds, Jason Robards, home.

Inside his bungalow he puts on water for coffee, and as it heats he fetches a notebook and pencil from his suitcase. He could try and sleep, but he has an idea that he can make the disgust he feels about lying to Sylvia work for him: he's going to write. But it won't really be writing, he thinks, cautious as a hunter stalking deer. I'll just bullet-point some ideas. It has been so long since he has written anything that the simple act of opening the notebook – old but unmarked, always to hand in case this moment should arrive – is exciting.

Seated at the small kitchen table, steam curling from his coffee, the white page before him feels not like a barren waste, as he feared, but a field of possibility. What starts here as pencil marks, he thinks, has the potential to become rooms of laughter like the one he left a couple of hours ago. All he needs to do is begin. Just begin.

He cannot do it. As if pencil and page are magnets with the same polarity, they refuse to meet. In desperation, Andy thinks of the advice an older comic once gave him, that when he had trouble coming up with new bits he would write out his old stuff first until, sooner or later, new material started to flow. But amnesia has taken hold. He can't remember a single bit. He tries visualising old shows, when he was a real comic with his own material;

he can see a room from his vantage on the stage: a dented microphone head, mildewed brickwork, a neon sign above the bar at the back of the room – he always looked for something like that to centre himself on as he turned his gaze to different parts of what was, beyond a few rows of upturned faces, virtual blackness. From out of this blackness he tries to force something. Anything.

He cannot do it.

There is a tapping. Andy stands up, walks through to the living room and hits the porch light switch beside the front door – big as an iPad, for old and shaking hands. He cracks the door and sees a thin old man in a dressing gown. The light catches a few filaments of hair that arc from his bald scalp. He is statue-still, squinting in the sudden light. His mouth begins moving but Andy cannot hear words, only strained breath. The old man's hands shake at his sides.

'Hello,' says Andy, opening the door wider. The old man is alone. 'Can I help you?'

'I'm back, Joe,' the man says. His eyes are rheumy and searching. He takes a step backwards, then forwards.

Andy sighs. Now this interruption has come he feels certain that he was on the verge of a major breakthrough.

'Can I help you?' he says. 'I'm actually in the middle of something, so . . .'

The man waves his hand as if to say, 'Go right ahead,'

but stays standing on the threshold. Andy suspects if he closed the door in his face he would find him there, still muttering, when he opened it again in the morning.

Andy sighs more loudly, with resignation this time. 'You want to sit down? You want a drink or something? Cup of tea?'

'It's all bullshit,' the man says conversationally, then turns and sits in one of the wicker porch chairs that face each other beside the front door. He crosses his legs, letting a long, towelling-slippered foot dangle.

Andy looks up and down the street. The bungalows stand silver in the moonlight. The humidity feels like a large hand being held just in front of his face. The old man hums to himself. Something stirring. Maybe Beethoven.

'Glass of water?' Andy says.

The man leans his head on a skinny fist and smiles.

Andy goes inside and massages his closed eyes, wondering what to do. He puffs his cheeks and presses air through his lips. He pours a glass of water from a jug in the refrigerator and takes it out to the man, who politely accepts it but then leans forward and looks around worriedly. He motions for Andy to sit down. As soon as he does the old man grabs his wrist with unexpected force.

'The tent's a broken river,' he says, shifting forward in his chair. His dressing gown flaps open and Andy can see his naked body deep inside it, further back, surely, than it should be: a thin white root supporting a tiny, creased pot belly. 'Understand?' the man says. 'Joe!' He looks more angry than confused. His grip on Andy's wrist tightens. He starts humming again, a surprisingly resonant sound coming from the back of his throat. His breath is sour. It smells like clubs before they open. As he hums, tears fill the old man's eyes.

'Hey, calm down,' Andy says, but the humming only grows louder. Andy looks around the porch and out onto the dark street, willing help to appear, but they are alone. The old man's face darkens with blood as he hums more forcefully. His grip tightens again. Tears streak his face and Andy, beginning to panic, pulls his hand away more violently than he intends to. The man falls forward onto the porch and kneels there, sobbing. His slippers have fallen off and lie arrowed behind him. Andy bends over and lifts him up, moving him back to the chair. For a few moments the man's scalp rests against Andy's cheek. It smells of talc and, beneath that, a repellent mustiness. He weighs very little. Cradling him makes Andy think of holding Marcus, and Tim before him, of rocking them to sleep or soothing away an injury. The old man begins to softly snore as Andy leans him back in the chair, the wicker creaking.

#

Andy collects a hire car and drives to the bachelor party. He has no idea how these people heard of him, he has never played one outside New York or New Jersey before. He has overdone the paint stick, and works his mouth and eyes to see what kind of movement he can get. His face feels as if it's going to crack open like an egg. From the rear-view mirror a singed, startled man stares back.

'You have reached your destination,' the satnav states. He is on a dark country road. His appearance is supposed to be a surprise, so he stays beside the car and calls Todd, the best man, to tell him he's here. The house is old, a Spanish revival mansion screened from the road by banyans, their trunks smothered by Virginia creeper.

Todd is tall, muscular, about thirty years old. He is wearing a polo shirt and khakis. His stride is so assertive that he is either extremely poised or extremely wasted. The latter, Andy decides.

'Nice place,' he says, holding out his hand.

'It's not mine,' Todd says. He sounds agitated. He is smoking a cigarette with quick, urgent drags. He flicks it away into the dark half-finished and pulls a pack from his pocket. He points it at Andy like he's changing channels.

'No thanks,' Andy says, retracting his unshaken hand. 'I quit.'

Todd laughs loudly, a sound like a child mimicking a machine gun.

'Just wait till I start telling jokes!' Andy says, but Todd doesn't seem to hear. He pinches a cigarette from the pack and flicks his lighter. He sucks furiously, the lighter's flame several inches below the cigarette's tip. One eye screwed tightly shut, he stares at Andy with the other.

'Things all good here, Todd?' says Andy, beginning to dread an entire room of Todds. Todd has taken the cigarette out of his mouth and is holding it in the lighter flame. He ignores Andy as he stares at the jerking cone of fire. He is concentrating so hard Andy almost expects the metal of the lighter to bend, or the cigarette to erupt into a bouquet.

'Dude!' Todd says as if waking from a trance. He pockets the lighter and tosses the charred cigarette onto the lawn. 'Let's get inside. Mike'll freak when he sees you. He fucking loves Johnny Kingdom.'

'Good to hear,' Andy says.

Todd pauses. 'What's that accent?'

'English.'

'Weird,' says Todd. He stares down the darkened road for a few seconds, stares hard as if he might see Europe at the end of it, then gives Andy a broad, insincere smile. 'Come on inside.'

Todd leads the way to the house. He lights another cigarette, the smoke shredding itself in the porch light. He pushes the door open and waves Andy into a large, terracotta-tiled hallway.

'Is it the strippers?' asks the man, as tall and solid as Todd, who emerges from a door on the right. Beyond it Andy hears loud dance music and shouting voices, all male.

'How many people are here?' Andy says.

Todd looks at him, bewildered. He draws on his cigarette and says, 'Twenty? Twenty. No, it's not the strippers. It's Johnny.'

'Oh,' says the other man. His cap reads 'Marlins' in black edged with turquoise. Beneath its curved bill his bloodshot eyes stay fixed on Andy as he lifts a red plastic cup to his mouth.

Todd looks at nothing for a moment, his eyes empty, then he comes back to them. 'Brian,' he says, 'take Johnny upstairs. You need to get dressed, right?'

Andy nods.

'How long you need?'

'Twenty minutes?'

'Great, perfect,' Todd says. 'Put him in the games room and give him whatever he needs.' He taps his nose with his finger and smirks at Brian. Brian shrugs.

They go up a broad tile staircase and down a hallway that runs the length of the house. Up here it is quiet. Only the muffled thump of music carries from below.

'Good party?' Andy asks Brian's back.

Brian shrugs. 'S'OK,' he says. He is round-shouldered, his muscle slackening into fat. He moves reluctantly, as if carrying out the last chore of a long day. He takes Andy all the way down the hall and through a door into a large bedroom with a king-size double bed, and a dressing table in front of a tall window. Andy can see a balcony through a pair of narrow glass doors. On the dressing table stands a lump of cocaine the size of a tennis ball. Around it lie little scars of powder, sharply outlined against the dark brown wood.

Brian crosses the room. 'Want to hit this?' he says, bending down and herding smaller lines into something the length of a microphone.

'That's a lot of cocaine,' Andy says.

Brian considers the lump. 'You should have seen it before,' he says. He looks at Andy. His eyes slowly cross and uncross. He offers a rolled-up bill and Andy is tempted, in spite of what it does to him. The last time, at a party on Long Island before the kids were on the scene, he wrestled an old college friend of Sylvia's and woke up under a bush.

'Not when I'm working, thanks.'

Brian shrugs and inhales the line in two wetly rippling snorts. He straightens and lets out a wolf howl, a thick vein in his neck pulsing. Andy lays his suit bag and holdall on the bed and starts unpacking.

Brian leaves. Todd walks in with a bottle of vodka in one hand and a cigarette in the other, trailing a thin, reptilian boy behind him. Todd points at the boy and looks at Andy. 'Martin,' he says, 'the groom's little brother.' Martin, who is perhaps eighteen, looks hunted, and sniffs powerfully as he approaches the dresser. Todd is shaving the lump with a credit card.

'Bathroom?' Andy asks, his outfit draped over his arm.

'On the left,' says Todd, his face low over the table as he dices the coke. As Andy crosses to the door, Martin looks at him with a strange intensity and slowly shakes his head.

In the bathroom Andy changes his clothes, puts on his wig and concentrates on moving through the gateway between himself and Kingdom. Outside the door he hears people come and go, laughter, another of Brian's wolf howls. He is sticking on his mole, inhaling the sweet sherry odour of the spirit gum, when someone bangs on the door. 'Just a minute,' Andy calls. Another powerful series of blows shakes the latch. He checks himself in the mirror: Johnny's here. He opens the door. There is no one there. 'Hello?' he says, in Johnny's voice. There is no reply. He walks into the bedroom and looks around. He looks at the coke, scarred and pitted like a meteor. A credit card and a rolled-up note lie beside it. The end of the note is flecked with blood. Two small lines sit at a slight angle to each other. He sees the old man's slippers on the porch, their towelling worn at the toe and heel. He feels like curling up on the bed and sleeping, hiding from everything, but that's Andy. Johnny wants to get down there and make those fuckers laugh. And Johnny would never let free blow go unsnorted. He touches his tie knot and stretches his neck. He takes a note from his wallet, rolls it and sniffs the powder, half up the left nostril and half up the right. He steps backwards and flops down on the bed. He stares at the ceiling and works his lips. They feel carbonated. A chill lump gathers at the top of his nostrils. His face goes numb, sweat springs from his fingertips, the bed sheet feels coarse and staticky against them. *A fraction of the talent*, the words chatter through his head, *at a fraction of the price.* He repeats the sentence to himself in a rhythm like the movement of a train. An old Mitch Hedberg line comes back to him: *I used to do drugs. I still do, but I used to, too.* He died, of course. Of a drug overdose. 'Motherfucker,' Andy says aloud. His vocal cords pop. Speaking feels unusual, but good.

Todd reappears and moves straight to the dresser. He leans down and, a moment later, rears up. 'Time to go,' he says, pressing his nostrils shut and blinking back tears. They walk along the hallway and back down the stairs. A big band fanfare struts from the stereo as Andy comes into the large, long living room. The furthest wall is open to the night, and it is so dark outside the house might be suspended in space. There are cheers and shouts, and a man so drunk that he moves like a marionette is pushed in front of Andy. 'Mike?' says Todd, beaming and clapping Andy on the shoulder. 'Meet Johnny.' Mike has a slash of cherry-red lipstick running from the midpoint of his lips to his left ear. Bruise-purple eye shadow has been smeared around his eyes, giving him a look of end-stage disease. The eyes themselves are almost entirely pupil. He is dressed in the same khakis and polo shirt outfit as nearly everyone else, which makes the make-up seem more obscene than fun. His lips are pulled back from his teeth in what might be an expression of happiness or horror.

'Mike!' says Andy, as Johnny, 'it is an honour to perform for you tonight. Great crowd you got here. You look in their eyes, they could almost be human.'

Todd sniggers but Mike says nothing, only bobs his head.

'Anyway,' Andy says, patting his shoulder, 'let's get this show on the road.'

He stays at the top of the room while his audience gathers around the couches and armchairs that have been rearranged to face him. Martin, the reptile, is sitting next to Mike on a large couch, speaking urgently into his ear. Mike's head lolls like his neck has been snapped. Standing behind the couch Andy sees an older pair who must be the fathers, scarlet with alcohol, one bald and the other with cropped silver hair. Everyone is sniffing energetically and smoking with intent, some cigarettes but mostly cigars. The clouded air smells burnt. Bottles and plastic cups crowd every surface.

'I was with this girl,' Andy says, shouting to quiet the room. 'She loved me so much. "You're like nothing else, Johnny, you get me so fuckin' hot, Johnny." She was the girl of my *dreams* this girl.' He shrugs and shakes his head. 'But then I woke up.' They roar, all except Mike and Martin, who are both speaking now, their heads bent towards one another. Andy's eyes keep flicking back to them. In any audience he has learned to tell where the pockets of resistance are. 'My wife, she treats me like dirt,' he says, working his way into the rhythm. 'The other day I come home from work and some guy's outside my house stark naked. I say, "Where's your clothes?" He says, "Where's your work ethic? You're two hours early."'

At the end of each line, another convulsion. That simple, supple transaction Andy loves: words, then laughter. Time it right and the laughter starts generating its own energy, and it's that you want to tap, the pure stuff. The lines are just the tools you need to get to it. He sniffs, and shudders as the taste of ammonia floods his mouth. He hears laughter, but doesn't know what he just said. 'I told my wife,' he says, hoping he isn't repeating himself, 'I told her, "I'm seeing a psychiatrist. He says we should break up." She said, "I'm seeing a truck driver. He says the same thing."' Andy leans on the laughter for a moment, taking the chance to regroup, and it's then that the answer comes, like one of those perfect ad-libs that sometimes arrive as if beamed into him: the way out of Kingdom is through Kingdom. All this, the bachelor parties and retirement homes, Suzzy and Todd and the stink of clubs in the afternoon and dressing rooms stacked with cleaning supplies and being forty and other comics hating you, and Johnny looming over it all: this is the show Andy will write. He even knows the title: *Leaving the Kingdom*. He has no idea if it will be funny, but it will be his. His absorption in the idea is so complete that it takes him a few seconds to make sense of Mike launching himself from the couch and staggering towards him. He jabs his finger at Andy. 'Whoa, fella!' Andy says. 'What's wrong with this guy?' He leans around Mike's shoulder and mugs at the crowd, trying to keep the room on side.

'You come here . . . come here,' Mike is repeating, grinding the words out through his clenched jaw. His hand makes a staccato chopping motion.

'Mike,' says Andy quietly, speaking in his own voice as Mike sways in front of him, 'buddy. Don't be a prick.' As he speaks, Andy feels Mike's foot against his own. He can smell the booze on the younger man's breath, and trace each vein in his bloodshot eyes. Surprising himself, he lifts his foot and brings his heel down hard on Mike's toes.

Mike howls and shoves his fist into the thick frills on Andy's shirt. It isn't a punch, more a heavy placing. Andy puts his hands up on Mike's shoulders. People are around them, shouting. Mike launches his head towards Andy but his aim is off, his forehead only grazes Andy's cheek. Andy falls backwards and clears a side table with his arm. He is on the floor and someone is asking if he's OK. He lifts his hand to his face. 'Fine,' he nods, 'I'm fine.' Then Martin kicks him in the stomach, and as he curls up something slams hard into his head.

Andy drifts away from the noise and motion. He can hear a whine, like a neighbour's drill. He looks up. Todd has his arms around Mike. Brian is shoving Martin and pointing down at Andy. The fathers are standing above him. Andy can see powder at the edge of their nostrils, frost ringing a chain of black ponds. He looks at Mike in Todd's arms, placid now, almost asleep. He sees his mole pressed into Mike's forehead. Everything moves very slowly. Then Martin squirms past Brian and kicks Andy in the face and again in the stomach. Andy curls up. He feels dislocated from everything around him. He sees Martin fall to the floor, and then he feels himself being lifted and carried into the hallway. He is put in a chair and someone leans over him and says something. The door to the living room slams closed and he is alone.

His vision spins; a terracotta whirlpool. Images of the

last few minutes warp and scatter. He stands up slowly. The upstairs hallway seems longer and narrower than before. He goes into the bedroom and picks up his clothes, stuffing them into his holdall. He walks back down the hallway, faster now. He listens for someone coming upstairs but hears nothing except a buzzing that he thinks is in his head. He wipes his hand across his face and it comes away bloody. He walks downstairs, needing to lean on the wall. The living-room door is still closed; from beyond it he hears angry voices. He sees a pack of cigarettes on the hall table and snatches it on his way past. He walks out of the front door, down the driveway and back onto the dark road to his car. He starts the engine and speeds away. After a few miles he finds himself driving on a long, straight road with fields on either side. He pulls over into the yellow-white glare of a streetlight, the only light he can see. He grips the wheel tightly and tries to slow his breathing. A cry comes out of him but he swallows it. He gulps air like he has been pulled from the ocean. He presses the dashboard lighter. His face is hot. His body shivers. His stomach is cramping. His left eye is swelling shut.

His stomach flips, and he fumbles with the door handle and throws himself to his knees in the tall roadside grass. When he has finished throwing up, all he can hear is his ragged breath and, all around him, the loud, pulsing static of cicadas. The earth holds the day's warmth. Grass tips press lightly against his face. He tears a hank of grass and wipes his mouth with it. He fights the urge to curl up and sleep. Instead he stands, pulls off his wig and throws it into the black field. Next is the jacket, its dark shape swallowed by the emptiness beyond the glare of the streetlight. He levers off his shoes and tosses them, overarm, in arcs down the road, then drops his trousers and stamps on the cuffs as he pulls out each leg. He gathers them into a ball and pulls his arm back to throw, pain gripping his stomach, when he feels his phone in the pocket. He takes it out and drops the trousers to the ground. He wants to tell Sylvia what has happened. He wants to tell her his idea. He wants to tell her everything. In shirt, underpants and socks, in the middle of the spotlit road, he calls home.

EVA

Joe had thought he would never hear from Eva again. The email arrives nine years after he saw her last, sent from a hospital in Sweden by a doctor called Järnfors. One of this doctor's patients claims to be Joe's wife. He knew Eva had returned to Sweden, but had stopped wasting time wondering where she was living or what she was doing. Now, again, he knows. She is in a hospital in a town called Borås, in the west of the country, not far from Gothenburg.

Yes, Eva Dewar is my wife, Joe replies, uncertain how much the doctor already knows. *We are separated, and have had very little contact with each other for the past decade.* He includes his number, and the following day Dr Järnfors calls and tells him that Eva was admitted just over a month ago, 'in a highly distressed state. Our evaluation at that time,' she says, 'was psychosis.' Joe is distracted by the clarity of her voice. It is as if she is standing directly beside him in his kitchen, or somehow even closer than that: an inner voice, or an imagined one.

As if in response to the thought, the doctor begins to

talk about auditory hallucinations and schizophrenia – or at least she uses a word with 'schizo' in it. Schizo-something disorder. Joe reaches for his tablet to make a note, but only stares into the screen's soft glow, listening to the doctor describe the woman he thought had disappeared for good.

'What can you do for her?' he interrupts.

'We—' she begins, then clears her throat. 'We must proceed according to our current evaluation only, Mr Dewar. What I can say is that Eva has improved significantly since she came into our care. This desire to contact her family is, we feel, another positive step.'

'She hasn't wanted to see us for years,' Joe says.

'Well, she has asked to see you now,' the doctor says. 'You and,' she pauses, perhaps to read her notes, 'Marie. She says you are the only people she knows.'

Joe remains sitting in the kitchen until it is lit only by a streetlight. At some point he says, 'Call Marie,' and the dialling icon appears on the tablet's screen. What will he say? *Marie, we've found your mother. Marie, she's back again.* 'End call,' he says.

#

It was on their third date that Eva told Joe she had once tried to kill herself. They were sitting at the counter of a cramped, crowded tapas bar in Soho, and Joe had to lean in close to hear her. She didn't look at him, only stared down at her fingers splayed against the marble. Joe looked down too, following the oyster-grey veins that curled like smoke through the white stone.

Two years ago, she said, she threw herself off a bridge in Innsbruck. 'The Innsteg footbridge. I found it on You-Tube.' She laughed as if she was telling an embarrassing story about herself, some foolishness from her childhood. She booked a hotel nearby, she said, and when she arrived she unpacked her things very neatly, 'because that mattered, for some reason'. She left the hotel, crossed a busy street, walked halfway across the bridge, climbed the iron balustrade and stepped off.

'Going there – all the way from London – I felt better than I'd felt in months. Isn't that funny? I knew something was going to happen that would change everything. And when I decided to really do it' – she stabbed the counter – 'it was like solving a puzzle you've been stuck on forever. I was so excited I almost ran to the bridge.'

She fell ten metres into fast-flowing water and was washed downriver towards another, larger bridge. 'The current kept turning me around. I was pulled out but I'd swallowed so much water I didn't know much about it. Someone, I never found out who, gave me CPR. They told me in the hospital. I was there for a few days, I had to be

223

interviewed by a psychologist and I got a telling off from some policemen. They said they could arrest me but they let me go. As soon as they discharged me I flew back to London.'

'And then . . . Are you OK now? Sorry, that's stupid.'

'No, it's not stupid, I *am* OK,' she said, looking up from the counter and into his eyes. 'Something washed out of me in the water. I've never felt like that again.'

#

An image remained fixed in Joe's mind: Eva pulling herself up onto the bridge railing and letting herself topple. Over and over again he saw her fall. He didn't know anyone who had ever done something like that. He wanted to see her again. He invited her to a dinner at a pub in Lambeth, a birthday party for his friend Toby. He felt proud introducing her, his arm around her, wanting her to feel secure among these new people. When she smiled or laughed it seemed loaded with significance, a significance the laughter of others lacked.

There might have been two dozen people there, a long, loud table. Between the main course and dessert Joe was absorbed in conversation with Shelagh, Toby's girlfriend, when Toby reached across the table and tapped his arm. 'Think Eva's legged it, mate,' he said.

Confused, Joe glanced to his left and saw her seat was empty, her jacket gone. 'Just having a smoke or something,' Joe said, but he knew Toby was right. He slipped on his jacket as he left the pub. It was autumn, a still, crisp night. He headed towards Waterloo and found her a couple of streets away, almost at the tube. 'Where are you going?' he called.

She stopped and turned. 'Home,' she said. She looked miserable.

'How come? What's wrong?'

She squirmed her shoulders. 'Parties,' she said. 'Just needed to go.'

'OK,' Joe said, smiling, 'so where are we going?'

'No, Joe, you stay.' She tried a smile that veered into a grimace. 'I'll call you, OK?'

He watched her until she turned the corner.

'It felt like I couldn't breathe,' she said when he called her the next day.

'Sounds like a panic attack,' Joe said. 'My mum gets those.'

There was a pause. 'It's just something that happens sometimes,' she said.

'Have you ever talked to someone about it? Had it checked out?'

She laughed and blew out air. 'No,' she said, elongating the word. 'You think I should?'

'Ah, who needs doctors? You've got me now.'

#

Joe replays his conversation with Dr Järnfors. 'Schizo-affective disorder' is what she said. 'Search "schizoaffec-tive",' he says, and the screen blooms with information.

Schizoaffective disorder:
psychotic symptoms, similar to schizophrenia, and
mood symptoms of bipolar disorder
Show psychotic symptoms?
Show mood symptoms?

'Save search,' Joe says. He'll look another time.

#

A few months after they met, Joe and Eva were living together. Within a year they were married. It was a small wedding: just Joe's parents, his brother, Mark, his wife, Sally, and their two daughters, and Toby and Shelagh. Eva didn't invite anyone: she had no living family and no friends. She got on with Joe's friends without having grown close to any of them, and had a jokey reputation for going AWOL on nights out. 'Just keep an eye on her,

Joe,' Toby said on the morning of the ceremony, 'don't want her disappearing today.'

Writing his speech presented Joe with a challenge: he didn't know a lot about Eva. Her parents were dead, and there was a stepfather who either was or might as well be – she hadn't had any contact with him for years. Beyond that, all Joe knew about was their life together. Up to that point it had been enough. 'Memories are important, Joe-Joe,' his mum had said months earlier, when she had called him to unsubtly probe for information about this new girlfriend.

'We're making memories,' Joe told her. 'We'll make all we need.' He joked about it in the speech. 'My sleeper cell,' he called her. 'My international woman of mystery.'

But on the first night of their honeymoon, in Tunisia, eating dinner on a torchlit terrace with the palms clacking above them in the onshore breeze, Eva did tell Joe something she hadn't told him before, about the death of her mother and how sudden it had been.

'For a long time I couldn't let go of it,' she said. 'I'd wake up and see her on the bed, staring out of the window.'

'You still see her now?' Joe asked hesitantly, not wanting to seem too eager to know.

'Never since Innsbruck,' Eva said. 'I'm done with all that thinking about death. I'm more interested in life.' She smiled and lifted her cognac in a toast. 'Life with you.'

#

Joe types 'Borås'. He swipes around the town centre, then searches for the hospital. He finds it on the outskirts of town, a nondescript white and grey building six storeys tall. Borås looks more or less how he expects a Swedish town to look based on his very limited knowledge. He once thought they would go there, that Eva would want to show him the country she came from. But when he suggested it, not long after they were married, she said, 'I never want to go back there again. Never.'

#

The summer Marie turned three they went back to Tunisia. The company Joe worked for was growing fast and the hours were long, and he felt like he was missing seeing his daughter grow up. He loved having time to muck around in the water with her, or read storybooks and eat ice creams by the pool. Eva was quiet, but seemed happy enough. She grew addicted to harissa, bowls of which stood on every cafe and restaurant table. 'In Sweden when I was growing up,' she said, scooping the red paste onto a piece of bread, 'pepper was as exotic as it got.'

'What kind of stuff did you eat?' Joe asked, smiling.

'In Sweden?' Eva said, the bread hovering by her mouth.

'Yeah, when you were a kid.'

'You don't want to hear about that,' Eva said. 'Marie, nej!' The little girl had dug her fingers into the harissa, and was lifting them to her mouth.

'I do want to,' Joe said.

Eva, wiping Marie's fingers clean, glanced up at him, looking flustered. 'Maybe later,' she said.

He thought about it for the rest of the afternoon, throwing Marie around in the surf and chatting about nothing in particular over dinner, which they ate early, before Marie's bedtime. That night, while Eva sang Marie to sleep, he sat on their balcony drinking wine. He didn't notice how fast he was drinking. When Eva appeared and he poured her a glass he was surprised to see how little was left, and how clumsy he had become.

'She's OK?' he said. He had to make an effort not to slur his words.

Eva nodded.

'So tell me,' he said. Far below, in the darkness, he heard the sea turn on the beach.

'Tell you what?' Eva said, sipping her wine and stretching in her chair.

'About you. Sweden. Before you met me. Whatever.'

'Joe, I'm tired.'

'What about the book?'

'The book?'

229

'The book,' Joe said, becoming exasperated. 'That travel guide, the one you treat like it's the Bible.' She would read it while Joe swam and played with Marie, completely engrossed.

There was a long silence before Eva answered. 'It belonged to my mother,' she said. She was looking down at the table, her hands in her lap.

'And?' Joe said, making an effort to sound curious rather than angry.

Eva put a hand to her face. She rubbed the heel of her hand left and right across her forehead, her fingers splayed. 'That's enough, Joe,' she said.

'Eva!' Joe brought his hand down hard against the wooden slats of the table. Startled, Eva stared at him. He slumped back in his chair. 'Why the fuck can't you talk to me?'

Her eyes dropped to the tabletop again.

'Aren't we happy?' he said quietly. 'Don't I make you happy?'

She stood and he reached for her, but she pulled her arm away. She walked to the balcony door, a breeze lifting the wrap around her shoulders; for a moment it waved behind her like a cape.

Joe slapped his glass of wine off the table. It smashed against the balcony wall. Eva stopped and looked back at him, then opened the door and stepped inside. A minute later Joe heard the room door closing. A minute after that, leaning over the balcony railing, he saw her leave the hotel, cross the empty road to the beach, and merge with the darkness.

#

As summer became autumn, Eva picked up no new work. She wore her robe over her pyjamas when she walked Marie to nursery, and was often still dressed that way when Joe came home at night, lying on the couch watching TV while Marie played on the floor beside her. When she finally did get a few days' work at the beginning of October, he came home on the first day of her contract to find her in her pyjamas, the lights off, the room flickering as she switched between channel after channel, never staying on one for more than a few seconds. The volume was so high she hadn't heard Joe come in. The day's litter lay scattered across the coffee table: a crumb-speckled plate, the black bowl of a microwave meal, a flattened crisp packet. The room was stale with the smell of tobacco. On the floor he saw Marie watching something on the iPad, her hair a wash of shifting colours as Eva switched and switched again.

Joe scooped Marie up and carried her through to the kitchen, asking her if she'd had anything to eat. He kicked the door to the living room closed to block out the noise of the TV, and sat with her while she ate a pot of yoghurt. He took her upstairs, brushed her teeth and read her a story. He stayed with her until she was asleep. Then he went downstairs, opened the living-room door, switched on the light, snatched the remote from Eva's lap and turned off the TV. The sudden silence left a shocked echo in the room. Eva continued to stare at the screen, her jaw jutting obstinately.

'Why didn't you go to work today?'

'Not now, Joe,' she said, still looking at the TV.

'"Not now"? When?' She didn't answer, and he moved between her and the TV. She looked up sullenly.

'Later,' she said. 'OK?' As she spoke, tears came into her eyes. She squeezed her lips together, the skin around them whitening, but she couldn't stop the sobs. A long, trailing cry came from her. Joe sat beside her and held her for a long time, her legs across his lap, his hands smoothing her hair. They didn't speak; each time he tried to say something she shook her head, and pressed her face more tightly still into the space between his neck and shoulder.

#

The night after speaking to Dr Järnfors, Joe lies awake thinking about Eva. He is with her in Innsbruck, a shadow at her back. She ascends a staircase to a hotel room and carefully unpacks her clothes, diligently dividing her small supply of tops and skirts and underwear. The room is filled with the sound of traffic: narrow French doors open onto a barred ledge of a balcony that looks out, across a busy street, to the river. The sky is blue; it's a warm day in late summer.

She goes downstairs, hands in her key and leaves the hotel. She moves along the street with purpose. She crosses to the riverside, and for a few minutes she walks above it, against its flow. Joe has input start point and end point and scrolled along the street many times; he knows it's a three-minute walk from the hotel to the Innsteg Bridge, beside the rushing waters of the Inn.

The guardrails on the bridge are lattices of wrought iron painted green. As she crosses the bridge, looking down at the wooden boards at her feet, she runs her hand along the top of the guardrail, scudding over the half-sphere rivets that bulge from its surface. When people pass in the opposite direction she politely makes way. Halfway across, without breaking stride, she turns towards the downriver side of the bridge, puts her foot into one of the diamond openings in the latticework, lifts herself up, swings one leg over, then the other, and attempts to step out of her life. Joe follows, but he drops from the bridge only to return to the bed that, long ago, was theirs.

#

One sunny winter weekend Joe took Marie to Lewes. Eva had asked him to get out of the house at weekends, which he was happy enough to do. Why would he want to be there when all she did was lie on the couch, or sometimes shamble to the patio doors to smoke a cigarette? 'The same,' she would say when he asked her what she had done that day. Whenever he asked a question, whatever it was, she looked pained. When he shouted at her, which was often, she was impassive. Civil communication between them had dwindled almost to nothing.

Sometimes Joe took Marie to his parents in Hampshire, sometimes to Mark and Sally in Kent. This weekend was the first time he had been to see Toby and Shelagh since they had moved to Lewes the previous summer. That night Joe and Toby stayed up late drinking wine. Toby had a daughter a year younger than Marie, and they compared levels of tiredness and the small, amazing things each girl was doing.

'And Eva's still no better?' Toby finally said. Shelagh had asked after her at dinner, but the conversation had quickly moved on. Joe had been waiting for the question to be asked again, in less avoidable circumstances.

'She's OK, she's OK,' Joe said. 'She's got her problems but y'know; we're getting there.'

'Is she working?'

'Not right now, no. She's not ready for that right now.'

'Is she seeing someone?'

For a moment Joe thought Toby meant an affair. He laughed and shook his head. 'No, she's not. We've talked about it but . . . y'know. Things with her mum. She resists any kind of . . . medicalisation of things. And hey,' he smiled, 'she's got me, right? And Marie.'

'Yeah, mate,' Toby said, tipping his glass towards Joe. 'What woman could want or need more?'

They touched glasses, drank and fell silent. Joe peeled the label off the last bottle Toby had upended into their glasses.

'But y'know . . .' Toby said.

'What?'

'Well, a pro, a doctor or someone . . . She might be able to tell them things she can't tell you.'

'She can tell me anything. She knows that.'

'Course she can! Course she can! But sometimes it's, it's the people who're closest it can be hardest to tell.' Toby leaned over the table and spoke more quietly. 'Some of my shit . . . I just don't want Shelagh to have to deal with it, you know? Or you. Or anyone who isn't getting paid to hear it.'

'What shit?'

Toby winced and waved his hand. 'Not the point, just

. . . Just don't assume she'll sort herself out. Doesn't always go that way.'

It was dark the next afternoon when Joe and Marie turned onto their street. Eva was outside, wearing only her pyjama jacket, which barely covered her backside. She was pacing on the pavement outside the house, her breath streaming in the cold air, her skin yellow in the streetlight. As they got closer, Joe heard her repeating something again and again.

'They've arrived,' she was saying. 'Nothing's ready, they've arrived, they've arrived.'

'Eva,' Joe said, 'Eva,' but she didn't seem to hear his voice. When he took her arms to stop her pacing, she seemed not to recognise him at all. The stink of gin was coming off her, a smell that had made Joe recoil since the first time he ever drank himself sick. 'Go inside, Marie,' he said.

'Mamma,' Marie said, reaching up for Eva's hand. 'Mamma, it's cold.' Eva remained rigid in Joe's arms, looking around her in confusion.

'Marie, inside!' Joe said. 'Everything's OK, I just need to talk to Mum.'

Marie took a few steps backwards, then turned and went through the front door, which stood open to the cold night. It looked like every light in the house was on. 'Eva,' Joe repeated, 'it's me. It's Joe. I think you've had a bit too much to drink.' His voice seemed to calm her to an extent, and he was able to lead her off the street towards the house. His foot sent something skidding along the path – one of their landline handsets – and looking around he saw a number of other things strewn in the bushes that boxed in the small front garden: snapped cigarettes, a pair of knickers, a washing-up glove, balled pages from a magazine. A stack of plates had been dropped beside the front door, the bottommost plates smashed and the upper ones leaning haphazardly. When Joe shut the door behind them Eva began pacing again, walking up and down the length of the hallway.

Marie watched from the doorway to the living room. 'What's wrong, Mamma?' she said.

Joe knelt down beside her. 'Mum's not feeling well,' he said. 'The walking helps her feel better.'

Marie looked like she was about to ask another question, but didn't say anything. She watched TV while Joe persuaded Eva to come upstairs with him and lie down in bed. She fell asleep almost immediately and didn't stir for the next twelve hours. When she woke she didn't remember anything about what had happened. She remembered having a few drinks, but that was all. She tried to laugh it off, but Joe couldn't do the same. If she had sat at home and got drunk enough to black out that was a problem in itself, but he didn't think what he had seen was drunkenness.

Later that week Eva got up in the middle of the night and went downstairs. When he realised she wasn't coming back to bed, Joe got up to look for her. He watched her through the living-room doorway, her face blue from the TV. Bundled in a blanket, her legs tucked beneath her, she seemed to him like an animal in its den. Her eyes were staring, and it was difficult to tell if she was entranced by what she was looking at, or by something only she could see. He had no idea what was going through her mind. 'Eva?' he called softly, then again more loudly. Nothing.

Eva left their bed again the next night, and the night after that. Then she started making her bed up on the couch. She said she didn't feel able to drop Marie off in the morning or collect her in the afternoon, so Joe did the mornings and hired a childminder to take her until he got back from work.

It was within a few weeks of these new arrangements that Joe first slept with Gwen, his finance assistant. It was month end and the financial controller was away on her honeymoon, so Joe needed to put in a few late nights. Given Eva's state, Joe's parents had picked up Marie and taken her down to Hampshire for a long weekend. Unexpectedly, Eva protested against this arrangement, although she had said nothing when it was first suggested. 'I don't like her staying with them,' she told Joe while he was packing Marie's things.

'Why not?' Joe said, taking a handful of dresses from the wardrobe.

'They tell lies about me,' she said, shrugging as if what she was saying was common knowledge.

'What are you talking about, Eva? They love you.'

She smiled and shook her head pityingly. 'They despise me,' she said, as if talking to a child. 'They always have.'

But she let Marie go, and when, on the Friday night, Gwen suggested a drink, past nine and with the rest of the team already gone, he eagerly agreed. Better that than going home to Eva bundled up on the couch in a room that smelled of cigarettes and a body that had been cooped up too long. They went to a pub around the corner from the office, a sprawling place that was always deserted on the irregular occasions Joe went there. Paying for a bottle of wine at the bar, he realised he didn't really know Gwen at all. She had been at the company for three months, had just passed her probation, but they didn't work closely together. He knew she was from Leeds, and that he found her accent attractive. Found her attractive. Sitting at their corner table he asked the standard questions – how she was enjoying the job; what made her choose a finance role; was she going to take her accountancy exams? – but she didn't want to talk about any of that. She wanted to talk about him, and although he knew it was a bad idea he told her about Eva and the problems they were having.

'I don't know what to do, Gwen. I've tried everything.'

'She needs to see someone,' Gwen said.

'She won't.'

'She should. My uncle David had – *has* – depression and tried to tough it out for years – there's a Yorkshireman for you. He reckons going to see the doctor and getting pills was the best thing he's ever done.'

'He got better?' Joe topped up Gwen's wine. He felt drunk.

'Totally, yeah,' Gwen nodded. 'It was like, "Oh, David's back." Like this person you'd missed for so long suddenly walks back through the door and you're like, "All right."'

'That's it,' Joe said. 'That's exactly it. I know she's somewhere in there and I want her back.'

'Oh Joe,' Gwen said, putting her hand on his arm. 'Chin up.'

Leaving the pub, stepping into the frigid air, Gwen muttered, 'Fuck! It's freezing!' and moved against him. His arm went up to her shoulder. He squeezed it, and rubbed his hand up and down her arm. She squirmed against him, looked up, and they were kissing. Kissing her warm, winey mouth, the quick probing movements of her tongue, felt extraordinary. 'Take me home,' she breathed, and they were on each other like teenagers in the back of a black cab all the way to Hackney. It was when they stepped into her darkened flat, and she told him her housemates were away, that he thought what a terrible idea this was. But then she rolled down her tights and straddled him on the couch and he wasn't thinking any more. He carried her into her bedroom, or tried to – she slipped off him halfway there, and hopped along on one foot for a few steps, her other leg still hiked up, his hand gripping the underside of her thigh, before she pushed herself away from him and half-ran the last few steps to the bed. He hurriedly took off his clothes while she, on all fours on the bed, searched her bedside drawer. She rolled a condom onto him and guided him inside her. It had been so long that he feared he would come instantly. He tried to distract himself, staring at the iron curlicues of her bedstead, but when she gasped his name and dug her nails into his arms he couldn't hold off. He bore down on her, moaning in a way that sounded ragged and pained, but he was helpless to stop making the horrible sound. He pressed his face harder into the pillow to stifle it. 'Hey,' Gwen said, a hand in his hair, stroking his head. 'Hey, hey.'

When he woke up the green digits of the clock radio read 02:34. Gwen was snoring lightly. He picked up his clothes and got dressed in the living room, shut the door quietly behind him and walked down a cold stairway lit by a bright, flickering bulb. His head throbbed and his mouth felt coated in something foetid. Gwen lived off

Kingsland Road, busy at this hour, so there was no trouble finding a cab. Half an hour later he was turning his key in the lock as quietly as he could, the blood roaring in his ears. He heard voices, and saw the TV's shifting light reflected against the white of the living-room door. He edged towards the doorway and peered into the room. Eva was asleep, the remote clutched in a hand that dangled off the couch. He slipped it from her loose grip and switched off the TV. In the quietness he heard her breathing and thought of Gwen asleep in her bed across the city. His prostate throbbed. His penis was sticky, stuck in a tight spiral. He had been trapped, he thought. Forced into this. He felt sick. He wanted to go to bed and not get up for days, weeks. However long it took for everything to go back to what it had been like before. Eva's foot had escaped the covers. Joe tugged her duvet over it and left the room.

#

Joe used to spend a lot of time thinking about what he could have done differently and now, with Eva returned to reality, he is going over things again. With hindsight it is maddeningly easy to identify the things he got wrong, all the signs he ignored. He thinks he can even pinpoint the dividing line between hope and hopelessness to a specific weekend, although at the time it had felt like progress. It was Sally who gave him the idea. She had surprised Mark with a trip to Ghent the previous winter. 'It's romantic, Joe,' she said. 'Eva will love it. We can take Marie and you two can have some time for each other.'

Eva said no at first, but Joe asked her to think about it. He somehow thought if she agreed it would reset things after that terrible night with Gwen and give them a new start together. When he saw her poring over her old European travel guide he knew she had decided.

It shocked Joe to realise how strange it was to see Eva outside, away from her couch. She had put on weight and her skin was pallid and oily. She had never worn much make-up, had never needed to, but now Joe found himself wondering if it might make her feel better about herself if she did. He didn't say it, though. In fact on the Eurostar they barely said a word to each other about anything, spending most of the time reading. From Brussels they caught a half-hour connection to Ghent across flat farmland. Joe felt nervous: it was so strange to be alone together, on holiday, after the difficulties of the last six months.

They rode a tram to their hotel, past ornate buildings and across broad, empty canals, their surfaces choppy in the fresh spring wind, the moored boats rocking at the quayside. Their conversation was awkward, as if they were on a first date, but arriving in the city seemed to help Eva slough something off. The more time that passed, the happier she became. At the hotel, in a room that looked across the water at the fairytale battlements of Gravensteen Castle, she flopped down on the bed and laughed, sticking her legs in the air and cycling them round and round. 'Let's get drunk!' she said.

'You're on,' said Joe.

'And eat! I'm starving.'

They left the hotel, crossed the bridge beneath the castle and were soon in the cobbled alleyways of the Patershol. They ate ribs at a cosy, cluttered place with books lining the walls and oilcloth covers on the tables. They drank a bottle of wine, and afterwards found a cavelike bar where Eva insisted on trying the strongest Trappist beer they could find.

'Hardcore,' Joe said. 'Think you can handle it?'

Eva stuck her tongue out at him and the barman put two goblets of dark beer in front of them. Eva lifted her glass and gulped at it. 'Mm,' she said, smacking her lips and looking searchingly towards the ceiling. 'I'm getting flagellation . . . sackcloth . . . abuse.'

Joe laughed. 'Isn't it more priests who're the abusers?'

'Ah, no, you're right,' she said. 'Monks only abuse each other, and good on them for that.'

They watched the people around them. Joe enjoyed them being in this tight space together, listening to other people's talk and laughter, away from that vile couch and the inane noise of the TV.

'It's nice to be here with you,' Eva said, as if she had read Joe's mind.

'It's great,' he said. 'It's only a shame Marie isn't here.'

Eva shrivelled in her seat.

'What's wrong?'

'Please don't,' she said.

'What do you mean?'

'Isn't it enough to be here with me?'

'No, course it is,' Joe said, confused. 'I just meant I like it when we're all together, that's all.'

'We're on holiday,' Eva said, 'let's forget all that.' She gulped her drink.

'All that'? Joe wanted to say more but stopped himself. He looked around the bar and saw a group of musicians setting up in the corner: a guitarist, a double bassist, a violinist and a drummer with a single snare on a stand.

'Look at that guy,' Eva said conspiratorially, leaning over the table and jerking her chin in the direction of a bearded young man in a hoodie seated near the musicians. 'Interpol.' She glanced from side to side and hissed, 'He's here for the monks.'

The band struck up in a hot jazz style, the violinist

twisting his melody above the guitarist's staccato strum. They swayed in their seats to the first couple of numbers, and when Joe came back from the press at the bar with another round of drinks Eva was dancing in the narrow space between tables – the place was too small for a dancefloor. They danced for a long time, and at one point Eva paired up with her undercover policeman, turning circles beneath his raised arm. They were still breaking into occasional moves on the walk back to their hotel beside the black mirror of the Leie, the spotlit stone of the Gravensteen doubled in the water.

The next day they took a boat trip along the canals, joined a guided tour to see the Mystic Lamb at St Bavo's, and spent a couple of blissfully empty hours outside a cafe drinking hot chocolate with brandy in the chill air, a wool blanket spread across their legs. Joe didn't mention Marie. When he texted his mum he did it covertly, and that evening, before dinner, he left Eva reading in their room while he went down to the street to FaceTime Marie before bed. 'Look at the canal, Pluff,' he said, turning the phone and panning it slowly around him. 'Look at the castle! A big, angry king lives in there.'

'Where's Mamma?' Marie asked when Joe blew her goodnight kisses. The phone was in her lap, and her long brown hair dangled down towards the camera.

'She's just having a rest,' Joe said. 'She sends her love.'

'Is she resting because she's sick?'

'No, this is a getting-better rest,' Joe said, but he didn't know if Marie had heard him because the connection failed, and he couldn't get through again.

That night, having gone back to the hotel straight after dinner, they had sex for the first time in nearly a year. Joe tried and failed to stop memories of his night with Gwen seeping into his mind as he moved above Eva, and as they rolled and she moved above him. Her face was pained, her eyes closed. She dug her hands into her hair and pulled it up, up, until it radiated from her scalp in thick strands.

'Look at me, Eva,' he began to say as she pumped up and down. He felt that she was somewhere else. He wanted her there with him. He needed to see her. 'Look at me,' he said, 'look at me.'

She didn't look, and when it was over she didn't open her eyes, only curled up and pressed herself against him, and fell asleep without speaking.

#

The night they got back from Ghent, Eva moved back into the bedroom. In the following days she started swimming and running. She pulled her bike out of the shed and went on long rides around the Heath. For Joe it was like seeing a blurry picture snap into focus, and not only because of the weight she lost: her eyes were brighter, her posture better. She started using her free time during the day to go to the cinema, or read books in coffee shops. 'It's about structure,' she said, an urgency in her voice. She took Marie to nursery in the morning and was usually out until it was time to collect her in the afternoon. Cancelling the childminder, Joe thought happily that the time they had spent together had reforged some broken connection. He started planning another trip, thinking that Marie could join them this time.

But before his plans got anywhere, Eva crashed. He came home one night to find her back on the couch, back in the pyjamas. The Eva of the last few weeks had disappeared, leaving this empty casing behind. 'I want to go away again,' she told him, her voice sapped of energy.

'We can do that,' Joe said, 'but I need to give work some notice.'

'No,' she said, 'on my own.' The next morning she was packing.

She flew to Turin with a plan to do some walking in Piedmont. Joe didn't expect to hear from her, and didn't ask her to stay in touch. Maybe a period of total separation would help. A fortnight after she left, with no idea when she would come back, Joe asked his parents if they could take Marie for a few days. 'Work's a nightmare,' he told his mum. 'I need the weekend to sort it out.'

That Friday Joe and Gwen left work separately and met up a few streets away from the office. They sat apart in the cab they took to Joe's house then fucked in the hallway. They ordered takeaway and lay in bed watching a film on Joe's laptop. They had only spoken once about what had happened at Gwen's flat. Joe had taken her for a coffee and apologised. 'I like you a lot, Gwen, but what I did was wrong. My family . . .' The words, so familiar from TV shows, sounded unreal to him, almost pointless.

Gwen said she didn't mind. 'I get it,' she said, smiling and shaking her head a little as she spoke. 'It's fine. I get it.'

Now they were in Joe's bed, entangled under a duvet eating Chinese food. He wondered what would happen if Eva walked in and found them there. Would she care? Would he? He didn't think so.

The feeling didn't last. He woke up in the morning groggy from wine and appalled to see Gwen in the spaces normally occupied by Eva and Marie. When she came out of the shower he told her he had stomach cramps and a temperature. 'Maybe the food last night,' he said. 'Are you OK?'

'Fine,' she said, towelling her hair.

'You should go,' he said. 'I'm really sorry.'

'You're joking. You're chucking me out? Now?'

'No! I said, I'm sick.'

'Course you are, Joe,' Gwen said, pulling on her jeans. 'Fucking classy too.'

'Gwen—' he began, but she raised her hand to silence him. As she snatched up her things he stood there holding his stomach – not caring how it looked, just wanting her gone.

She stamped down the stairs and opened the front door. 'Pathetic,' she said without turning, and slammed the door behind her.

Eva returned a month later, in early summer. She had bought Marie a gift, a carved shepherd boy from a place called Biella, but she wouldn't say anything more about her trip. She shared a bed with Joe again, but when he tried to embrace her she pushed him away.

Joe felt, somehow, that he didn't have any right to try and draw Eva out of her silence. It exasperated him, but he felt like he deserved it. He couldn't tell her about Gwen. He thought he could explain why it had happened, but decided he would tell her later, when she was better.

It was during dinner, more than a fortnight after Eva got back, Marie in bed and most of a bottle of wine gone, that she said, 'I'll tell you something if you want. About where I've been.'

'I'd love that,' Joe said. 'I didn't want to ask till you were ready.'

She smiled in a joyless way, warping Joe's hopefulness

into aggravation. Did every little interaction need to be so fucking hard?

'I was in Stresa,' she said, emptying the bottle into their glasses, 'on Lake Maggiore. It's perfect. Like someone's dream of what an Italian lake town would be like. All day long I could just walk the streets or sit on the shore. There was no timetable. No need to be anywhere.'

Joe felt the comment implicated him and Marie, but kept silent.

'I met some people there, other tourists. We were all in the same bar a few nights in a row, two couples and a man whose wife had died the year before. It was the anniversary of her death and they'd been in Stresa together so many times that he wanted to come back. That sounds morbid, but it didn't at the time. It seemed quite beautiful, actually.

'We used to meet around ten. Someone suggested having dinner together, so we arranged it for the next night. It was all very easy, very sweet. But I lay awake all that night. I'd said something terrible at the bar, I realised, and now everyone was laughing at me behind my back. Not just my companions – the whole town was against me.' Her eyes, unfocused, looked at the remains of their dinner.

'What did you think you'd said?'

'I have no idea, but what I was feeling was shame. Unbearable shame. And I heard this . . . this bell ringing somewhere in the town and I kept thinking how lonely it would be out on the lake, hearing that distant bell, and then I realised –' she paused and stabbed the table with her finger, '– *that* was where I deserved to be, stranded somewhere out there.'

'On the lake? Why?'

'As punishment. Punishment for the crime I'd committed. It was horrific to realise. I cried and I couldn't stop crying. If I hadn't been so terrified at the thought of leaving my room I would have run immediately.'

'What crime? What does that mean?'

'Before Stresa I'd been walking about twenty K every day,' Eva said. She massaged her temples and blinked once, twice. 'Maybe I was exhausted. But that night I couldn't sleep. The morning was a disaster. My body felt huge and slack. The sun on the lake was too bright. The water from the shower felt like nails in my skin. And there was that feeling of a punishment waiting just outside my door. Walking into the dining room for breakfast was like walking into court. I was convinced everyone was staring at me, and that they were disgusted by what they saw. It was unbearable. I took a ferry to the islands the town overlooks. Tiny, tiny islands, you've seen everything in an hour, but I spent the whole day on them, pacing up and down. I couldn't sit down. Couldn't be still. By the time I got back it was twilight, and all the windows of the town were yellow patches in this deep blue darkness they have there; it's like the lake seeps into the atmosphere.

'Of course I didn't go anywhere near the restaurant – I couldn't risk being seen. I found the grottiest bar, somewhere I was sure those people would never go, and I drank a bottle of wine. I felt calmer then.' She raised her almost empty glass to Joe and tipped the last of the wine into her mouth.

'Did you see them again?' he said.

'I made sure I didn't. I paid my bill that night and left very early in the morning. I took a train to Locarno and stayed for a week. I felt better there, a lot better. I didn't talk to anyone; it felt wonderful. Then up to Zurich, then home.'

There was a long silence. 'Was it like Innsbruck?' Joe said.

'No, nothing like it,' Eva said. She looked up to the ceiling, thinking. 'In Innsbruck I was calm, happy even. I'd made a decision; I knew what I was doing. Here I felt . . . fear.'

'Of what?'

'Of who knows what,' she said, slumping down with her fist supporting her head. It was difficult for Joe to tell if she was tired or just bored of the conversation.

'You have to see someone,' he said. 'A doctor, no more avoiding it.'

She leaned back in her seat and rubbed her eyes. 'You're right,' she said through a yawn. 'You're right, you're right. No point running away, right?'

#

The next day Marie's nursery called Joe to say that Eva hadn't collected her. He tried calling her when he was on his way, but it went straight to voicemail. When he and Marie got home the house was dark. There was a note on the kitchen table, a few lines in pencil on a torn piece of paper:

> *I need to be somewhere else for a while. You'll hear from me.*
> *Eva*

They didn't see her again for seven years.

#

Dr Järnfors's voicemail is brief. 'Eva has requested to see you and Marie, Mr Dewar. Will you come?'

#

Marie didn't understand what had happened. At bedtime she would ask if her mamma was coming home tomorrow. 'Not tomorrow,' Joe said, 'but hopefully soon.' She developed a superstitious attachment to the couch. 'That's Mamma's place,' she said if anyone else sat on it. Joe would have liked to burn the thing.

When it had become apparent Eva wouldn't be working for a while Joe had set up a direct debit to cover her expenses, so he knew she had access to some money. But it wasn't enough to pay for the travelling she was doing. A couple of months after her disappearance a postcard from Japan appeared on the doormat. A month later another arrived, from Canada. Sometimes two came in a month, sometimes one in half a year, but always from somewhere different: Mexico, Vietnam, France, Norway. He wondered what kind of work she was picking up along the way. The cards never said anything about it. They never said much at all.

Slovenia 21/04/12
You two,
The woods here are full of yellow morels. Mornings
are the best time.
Kisses, Eva

Rome 03/06/14

I hope London is behaving itself and being good to
you both. Rome is OK.
I am well.
Eva

Istanbul 19/02/16
Happy new year, have an amazing 2016 Marie &
Joe.
Eva

None was any longer or more informative. When the
first card arrived Joe thought about going to look for her,
but knew it would be folly.

'Where's Mamma now?' Marie asked at bedtime, in the
dim glow of her nightlight.

'Well, the last postcard was from Greece, wasn't it?'

'But that was ages ago. Where is she now?'

'I don't know, Pluff, but she'll let us know.'

'Why is she away?'

'Mum's not very well,' Joe said. 'She needs time to get
better.'

'But why is she going to all those places?'

'She's looking for something she needs.'

'What is it?'

'She isn't sure. I don't suppose she'll know until she
finds it.'

A pattern developed. When a card arrived, whichever of them found it on the mat would leave it propped on the kitchen table where the other would see it. Joe never brought it up but waited until Marie wanted to talk about it, usually a day or two after it came. 'Mum's in Finland,' she'd say, or Gran Canaria, or Warsaw. Then they would discuss whatever morsel of information the card contained – *The beach is always windy*; *I saw a firework competition*; *In the morning there is ice on the inside of my window* – and these became the only times they spoke about Eva. Marie was a thoughtful girl who had never chattered much, but Joe thought her reticence when it came to her mum was different. Deeper. An inability to speak more than unwillingness. He would never say it, but he sometimes thought it would have been better if Eva had died, like her own mother had. Then Marie would have been able to get on with getting over it.

But Eva had not died, and the day came when a postcard arrived with a picture of an apple orchard on the front. Joe thought it looked like an English scene, and as he turned it over the familiarity of the stamp sent a shock through him. Eva was living in Sussex, the card said, and she wanted Marie to come and visit her there.

#

Joe thinks the shock then was greater than what he is feeling now. Back then he thought, briefly, about not going to see her at all, but knew he couldn't do that to Marie. Now, though, he is certain he won't tell her he knows where Eva is. If he tells her that he's going away he'll make something up. He is convinced that it's better this way.

#

Eva didn't say why she had come back, or how she came to be living in Hurstpierpoint, a village at the foot of the South Downs. The house she was renting was near the station, a shabby end-of-terrace two-bed with the crisp remains of a dead ivy snaking across its exterior.

On that first visit Eva came to the door with a tin holding a charred square of sponge. 'I baked you a cake,' she said, talking to Marie. 'A recipe of my mamma's, only hers was edible.' They went to the pub on the high street for some food, and for an hour mostly listened to the talk of people around them. But despite the awkwardness it was friendly enough, particularly between Marie and Eva. They were so obviously alike now Joe was seeing them together again.

They went back to the house for a cup of coffee, and before they left Joe asked Marie to explore what she could of the overgrown garden so he could have a word with her mum. He watched Marie from the window, talking to herself and peering into the brambles.

'You look well,' Joe said.

'Thanks, you too,' Eva said.

'You feel well?'

'Good as I look,' she said, laughing a little.

'I need to know you're better, Eva. I need to know you're not going to run away again.'

'I am. I won't.'

Joe turned to look at her. She was smiling at him. 'You've felt better before,' he said.

'I don't like the way you're speaking to me, Joe.'

'Well I'm sorry about that, but she's what I care about,' he said, pointing out of the window and struggling not to raise his voice. 'She loves you, and I won't let you abuse that.'

Eva shook her head and looked away. 'You'll see,' she said. 'No point in talking.'

'Did you enjoy that?' Joe asked Marie on the drive back up to London. It was dark, the red stream of the A23 flowing ahead of them through the night.

Marie didn't say anything for a long time. Joe began to think she was asleep, but then she turned her head towards him. 'I loved it,' she said, before turning back to the dark fields beyond her window.

259

Joe remained wary, but everything Eva did indicated she was sticking around. She found work at a production house in Brighton and she got a puppy, a Boston terrier she named Loki.

Marie was an independent eleven-year-old: on weekday evenings she had to be at home, but at the weekends she made day-long plans with her friends. Each time an invitation to Hurstpierpoint came, though, she cancelled them.

After a few of these day visits, during which Joe stuck around to make sure Eva was well enough to look after Marie, he agreed to let her stay over every other weekend. In London he would only see her for a few hours between Friday and Sunday night; she was staying over at her friend Harriet's house, or sleeping half the day and rushing out of the front door as soon as she had dragged herself from her room and showered. In the evenings, when she was home, she was in her room or gazing into her phone, oblivious to anything else. But there was no Harriet to lure her in Sussex, and Joe suspected that even the excitement of her phone paled beside the novelty of Eva's return. He told himself he was being ridiculous, but as he drove down to Hurstpierpoint on a dull, cold Sunday afternoon – Marie complained she could take the train, but he insisted – he first envied then resented the mother–daughter bonding ritual he felt he was about to disrupt.

He called when he was getting close and beeped the horn when he pulled up. He didn't feel like going in today. The house depressed him, with its render that flaked like diseased skin and windows opaque with condensation in cold weather. Now the garden was a brown wasteland, while in summer it transformed into an impenetrable thicket of hairy nettles. Inside there was almost nothing of Eva's on show beyond some trinkets on the gloss-tiled mantelpiece and a few postcards stuck to the fridge door.

He wondered what she did when Marie wasn't with her. Was there a man? Men? She was still attractive. But Marie would have told him if there was anyone she knew about. He wouldn't ask Eva himself; since she came back they had both kept their distance. Marie was their common ground, a boundary beyond which neither of them, he was sure, wanted to stray.

The only other thing they spoke about was money. Eva asked Joe to cancel the direct debit he had left in place for years, and said she wanted to repay what she had spent. 'It was never a loan,' he said, 'I wanted you to have it.' But she insisted.

#

The drive from London to Sussex became so familiar that even now, so many years later, Joe feels he could do it blindfolded. He never let Marie take the train. 'It's our quality time,' he said, although the drives often passed in near silence, Marie absorbed in her phone. Sometimes, mostly on the Sussex-to-London leg, they argued. Joe wouldn't have admitted it at the time, but he was jealous. He had stayed and Eva had gone, so why did Marie want to be with her more than him? Now Eva is back, and wants to see Marie again, the old wounds are reopening. He is surprised at how keenly he feels them, and how relentlessly they drag him into the past. He remembers that autumn afternoon when his arrival felt like an indefensible intrusion. Whether it was real or not he felt waves of resentment coming off Marie, and neither of them spoke for the first part of the drive home.

'Did you get out with Loki much?' he eventually asked. It had been a wet weekend.

'Of course,' Marie said. 'An hour each day.'

'You and that dog must have covered every inch of the Downs,' he said. 'Canny move, getting him.'

'What's that supposed to mean?'

'What?' Joe said, playing dumb.

'What, you mean she got Loki for me? As, what, bait or something? That's twisted, Dad. Mamma loves that dog. She'd be all alone in that house if it wasn't for him, you know.'

'What did you get up to, anyway?' Joe said.

'Stuff.'

'That's not very informative, Marie.'

'Things!' she sighed, putting her foot up on the glove box and looking out at the twilit countryside. The way she pushed her jaw forward in anger reminded Joe of Eva.

'Foot,' he said. She returned it heavily to the floor. 'What things?'

'Which things.'

'What, which, whatever,' Joe said. 'What. Did. You. Do.'

'Went for walks,' Marie said, exasperatedly. 'Drank coffee. Talked.'

'What did you talk about?'

Marie didn't answer right away. Joe glanced over. She wasn't frowning or rolling her eyes as he expected, she was simply looking straight ahead. 'She told me about a trip to Spain. Catalonia.'

'When she was away?' 'Away' was the word they used. Joe was trying to think if a postcard came to mind.

'No. Before you guys met.'

His resentment flared. Something she'd never told him about.

'She's a *really* good storyteller, Dad.'

'She is,' he said, nodding.

'No,' Marie said, 'I mean *really* good. When she was

talking it was like I was there.' She laughed. 'You know, there was this man,' she began, then stopped.

'What man?' Joe said. 'In Spain?'

'It doesn't matter,' she said. 'Tell you another time.' She leaned back in her seat. Soon she was asleep, and didn't wake until they got snarled in traffic at Mitcham. When they got home she flopped on the couch, in her own world, messaging her friends – Eva among them, maybe, Joe thought. Later she stood, stretched, and with a mute wave went to bed.

#

Joe calls Marie but she doesn't pick up. He remembers the call he took from her a few months before. It was August and she and her boyfriend Matt were still in Edinburgh. They had decided to stay for the Festival, but even as he asked her if they'd seen anything good he saw how nervous she looked, and she interrupted him before he could finish.

'Dad. I'm pregnant, Dad. We're going to have a baby.'

Joe knew it was his turn to speak, but no words came.

She winced. 'Sorry. I was going to say it a bit more . . . measuredly than that.'

'Oh, Marie,' Joe said.

'That doesn't sound happy. Can you sound happy for me?'

'Of course I'm happy. But your studies. You aren't going to be a doctor?'

'Yes. I mean . . . I'm still going to be. Just, like, not as quickly or, I guess, uncomplicatedly as I thought.'

Joe covered his eyes with his hand and massaged his temples.

'Listen, Dad,' she said, stern now, 'this wasn't a mistake or something, OK? I wanted this to happen. This was my idea.'

She stabbed the screen, leaving Joe staring at his reflection.

\#

Eva cancelled the next visit to Hurstpierpoint at short notice, and a week later sent Joe an email explaining that she wanted Marie to have Loki, whom she had left with a neighbour. She had given notice on her house and paid her bills. *I feel something coming*, she wrote, *and I need to get away before it arrives*. Joe had never wanted to hurt someone so much. Fifty-three years old and running away. He didn't know how he was going to tell Marie, but when he saw her he realised she already knew. He tried to comfort her but she wouldn't let him. Nor would she show him what Eva had written to her. For several days they barely spoke, and when a parcel arrived for Marie containing Eva's old travel guide – with no note – she didn't talk about it. He never saw her look at the book.

Postcards began arriving again. They were all from Sweden, and came at set times each year: on birthdays and at Christmas. When Marie turned eighteen Eva sent her a silver bracelet. The message read *Love Mamma*. It was the first time Joe could remember seeing either word on anything she had sent them, and he wondered what that meant. Was she in a good place? Would she ever come back again? Marie wore the bracelet, but Joe knew she would have traded it many times over for the chance to talk to Eva. To tell her how well she'd done in her exams, and her plan to study medicine.

It made Joe feel proud that Marie was going to university, the first person in his family to do so. Proud and old. At fifty-four he had become the office elder, and he felt like it. Gwen had moved on years before, and each new finance assistant looked younger, like a school kid who had wandered into the office by mistake. He must have appeared ancient. His parents were growing increasingly frail. 'Your father fell,' his mum told him on the phone one Friday evening, and exactly a week later he heard his dad's voice, almost apologetic: 'Your mother fell.' The regularity of Eva's postcards marked the time. Occasionally, although less and less, Marie would ask why he thought Eva had gone, and why she wasn't coming back. For years

Joe had stuck to the script he formulated the first time she ran away: your mum's sick and she's working on getting better. He didn't believe it, and he didn't think Marie did either, but they let it be the thing they said about her. For some reason, though, the most recent postcard, a picture of a railway station in some bleak Swedish town with a quick *Happy birthday Joe, Eva* scribbled on the back, no different from so many others, had infuriated him. The postcards, it struck him, were less a way of keeping in touch and more a nagging reminder. *Miss me*, each one seemed to say. *Miss me. Miss me. Miss me.*

Late one evening, a few weeks before Marie left for Durham, Joe heard her come back from the pub and make her habitual journey from front door to fridge. He intercepted her there, entering the kitchen as Loki uncurled from his basket and skittered over the tiles. Marie dropped some ham on the floor for him.

'Good night?' Joe said.

Marie shrugged, then nodded, and folded a slice of ham into her mouth.

'Drunk?'

She rolled her eyes. 'Slaughtered,' she said, 'obviously.'

'Good. Need to get in training for university.'

'Har,' Marie said through a mouthful of ham. 'What have you been doing?'

'Watching rubbish on TV.'

'Really watching? Or sleeping in front of?'

'More sleeping in front of. Listen, Pluff, can I talk to you about something?'

'Don't call me Pluff,' she said, but distractedly. She was staring into the fridge, making her next choice.

'It's about your mum. I don't know if . . .'

'Has something happened?'

'No, nothing. Not that I know of. But then how would we know if it had? We aren't worthy of knowing what she's actually doing, are we?'

'Dad, don't—'

'I can't forgive her for what she's done to you, Marie. She's so selfish. So dishonest.'

Marie's head sank down, her hair obscuring her face. Loki circled her, claws tapping, eager for more food. 'But isn't she sick, Dad?' she said.

'She could still talk to us.' Joe spat the words. 'She could let us help her.'

'Don't shout at me,' Marie said, starting to cry.

He drew her into a hug. Her fingers gripped the back of his neck. He could still remember her doing that when she was little, carrying her downstairs in the morning, her knees in his armpits. She used to settle her head against his chest and clutch, clutch his neck. They stayed holding each other for a time. Loki lay at their feet, his tongue expanding and contracting with each breath.

Joe pulled his face from Marie's hair. 'I just want you to know, it's OK if you get angry with her sometimes, too.'

She snorted into his neck.

'What?'

'Cue the acoustic guitar,' she said, pushing away and rubbing her eye with the back of her hand. Speaking with an exaggeratedly Californian accent she said, 'This is, like, a life lesson? And we're, like, growing as people in our, like,' she wagged her fingers to create quote marks in the air, 'experience of adversity?'

'You're laughing at me,' he said.

'No, Dad. Or yeah, but in a nice way. It's not . . .' She rolled her eyes, looking for the words or the will to say them. 'I like the postcards, OK? I like them. It does me good knowing she's out there somewhere. She's still my mum, even if she's really, really shit at it. If it's all I'm going to get I'll take it.'

#

'Hello Dad.'

'Hey Marie.'

She moves the screen to show him her swollen belly. 'Hello from bump,' she says. '"Bump". Puke.'

'Soften up, daughter. You're going to be a mum, y'know?'

'Sexist,' she says, her face returning to fill the screen. 'Hello from offspring.' Behind her Joe sees grey sky and the upper branches of a rain-sodden plane tree.

'Edinburgh's Edinburgh, then,' he says.

Marie glances at the window and back. 'This thing'll be born with fins. Dad?'

'Mmm?'

'Are you OK? You seem a bit . . .'

'A bit what?'

'Don't know. You tell me.'

'I'm fine. Just busy. Actually I've got this thing I wanted to let you know about. I've got to go to Germany for a couple of days.'

'Germany?'

'Yeah. Conference. Grown men and women losing it over the latest billing software.'

'Wow! Sounds amazing. Shame I can't come.'

'It is. You'd absolutely love it. How's Matt?'

'He's fine. Playing rugby. Says hi.'

He had been worried about lying to her, but it was easy. It was to protect her, after all.

#

After Marie left for university they spoke once a week, and texted or emailed most days. He had access to some of what she posted online. He saw her in the holidays if she came back to London, but she often signed up for training courses, or volunteer placements overseas. He let her know when a postcard arrived, and held it up so she could see the picture on the front while he read out the message.

It was on one of Marie's rare trips home that Joe first met Matt, when she had been seeing him for just a few months. Joe took them to dinner. Matt, also a medic, had a very calm way about him, which Joe liked – he found himself imagining Matt explaining, in an utterly soothing way, that Joe's biopsy had uncovered rampant, inoperable cancer – but by the end of the meal he was bored of him. He was happy to let Matt talk, though, as it allowed him to look at Marie. He was so impressed by her, a woman now. 'My god!' she said as Matt plodded through the story of their first date, her elbows on the table and a glass of red wine clutched in her hands, 'Don't undersell it! It was a disaster, Dad. He was charm incarnate until we ran into his teammates outside the curry house. Then it was all chest-bumps and songs about arses and "Who's this fine filly?" Like bloody Wodehouse minus the wit. I wouldn't see him again until I'd had proof he could read. And that he recognised the stupidity of physically invasive initiation ceremonies. Or could pretend he did, anyway.'

At the end of the night Joe shook Matt's hand and said, 'Of course, no one will ever be good enough for my daughter, but I'm very happy to meet you anyway.' They all laughed. He seemed kind, which Joe thought was enough.

In the summer before her final year Marie went travelling around Europe with Matt, taking Eva's old travel guide with her. 'In case I fall through a wormhole to the 1970s,' she said. She was vague about where they were going, but Joe wasn't surprised when postcards arrived from at least two places he knew Eva had visited: Cadaqués and Innsbruck. The one from Innsbruck showed an old, colourised photograph of the town with the Inn given prominence, a single, distant bridge crossing it. Joe wondered, did Marie know what happened there? Had Eva ever spoken to her about it? He thought about all those weekends in Sussex. The strange thought occurred to him that his daughter knew more about his wife than he did.

He wanted to talk to Marie about the trip, but in the end – home for a single hectic day before returning to Durham – all she said was she had wanted to visit the places her mum had told her about. 'The way she spoke about them, Dad, do you remember?'

'Yes,' he said, thinking Marie had forgotten Eva shared some things only with her, and disturbed at the thought that neither of them could be sure how much the other knew.

#

Joe takes an early flight to Landvetter airport. He hires a car and drives east along a motorway cut through pine forest. It is only now, in the solitude of the car, that he grasps the reality of what is happening. Nervous, he turns the radio on for distraction and jumps as music roars from the speakers. He fumbles at the unfamiliar dashboard, and laughs as he begins making sense of the noise. 'Fucking Abba?' he says aloud. 'Are you kidding me?' He shakes his head and squeezes the wheel in his hands. He murmurs the melody, begins to half-sing words he had forgotten he ever knew, and as the verse flows into the chorus he lowers the window and shouts it into the freezing air.

The hospital where Eva is being treated is on the outskirts of town, at the edge of a birch forest. When Joe arrives he meets briefly with Dr Järnfors. She tells him Eva has been looking forward to his arrival, but asks him not to talk for too long, and to try and keep the conversation light. 'It can be very difficult to see people we have been close to after so many years apart,' she says. 'I do not want Eva to be disturbed by your visit.'

'Of course, Doctor,' Joe says. Does she think this is easy for him? Or that he's come all this way to chat about the weather?

A nurse leads Joe to a ground-floor cafeteria, its windows overlooking a courtyard with some bare bushes at its centre. The windows must be tinted; through them the grey day looks more like twilight than mid-morning. Aside from a couple of staff cleaning the tables the cafeteria is empty. Scatters of rain begin to blow against the glass. The nurse brings Joe a cup of coffee, and puts one across the table from him for Eva. 'Decaf,' she says, unsmiling.

'Both of them?' he says, but she ignores him, sits down a few tables away and pulls out her phone. A cluster of bubbles revolves on the black surface of the coffee.

Joe has his back to the cafeteria doors, and doesn't see Eva until she is right beside him. How old she looks. She is just the other side of sixty from him, but she could be fifteen years older than that. Her skin is yellow and deeply wrinkled. Her cheekbones are more prominent than they have ever been, even than when he first met her, only now they are not markers of beauty but indicators of approaching death. Between them and the way the skin around her eyes has shrivelled, it's her skull Joe sees first, her face second. Her eyes, those beautiful green eyes, have turned watery, unfocused and indistinct. Her mouth quivers and her hand flaps, searching for the tabletop as if she is blind.

'Hej,' she says, 'hur mår du?'

'Bara bra,' Joe says, remembering some of the Swedish she taught him when they first met. He had imagined back then that he might one day be fluent. It had never happened.

She says something more in Swedish, and Joe stares at her uncomprehendingly. Realisation animates her face. 'Förlåt! Sorry! I haven't spoken English in so long. I asked if you saw the zoo.'

'Oh, yes. I came past it on my way here.'

'I hear them, you know. The animals. Early in the morning, and sometimes in the middle of the night.'

The topic of conversation is unexpected, but she seems lucid. How old she has become, though, he cannot stop thinking it. Her thick hair has thinned and greyed. It is wet and combed, hanging straight down on either side of her face. She isn't wearing make-up, and the shape of her mouth and the sloppiness of her speech tell him she has lost some teeth. She is wearing a plain blue sweatshirt that is much too long for her, dark, loose cotton trousers and canvas slippers. She holds her hands out in front of her, fingertips touching, as if she is holding something very small and delicate. They shake – or rather vibrate: the movement isn't pronounced, but it is constant. They are liver-spotted, their veins raised.

'Time's ravages,' Eva says, following Joe's stare. 'With,' she adds, lifting her clenched hands to her mouth as if swigging from a miniature bottle, 'a lot of alcohol thrown in.'

'Where did you go, Eva?' Joe says.

She looks out at the frozen courtyard. Her sunken mouth creases into a smile, but not in a way that has anything to do with happiness. 'All around,' she says. 'I went all around. Wherever I could pick up some work. It seemed to help if I kept moving. Whenever I stopped moving everything became . . . too much.'

'You made enough money like that?'

'Not really. I had some savings but they ran out. But it wasn't so hard getting something, usually: shop work, washing dishes, anything. I picked blueberries in Värmland one summer, with the Vietnamese. That was hard work. They went on strike.' She looks down at the table. Her shoulders subside, as if she is exhausted. 'I took some charity. You meet some good people. And bad. Part of the time, for half a year maybe, I lived in the woods – down south, where it's warmest.'

'You camped?'

'Yes, camped. I had a little tent and a sleeping bag. I can build a fire, I can find mushrooms, I know which berries to eat. But I was never so far away from civilisation, really. Most of the food I ate was canned, not . . . ah . . .'

'Foraged?'

'Yes! My English is not good. Even my Swedish, I think, is going.'

It's true. In the short time they have been talking her speech has deteriorated. Maybe the booze has slowed her down, Joe thinks. Could she have had a stroke at some point? He will ask Dr Järnfors. He has noticed also that she fills the spaces between words with odd sub-vocalisations: quick bursts of humming that sound like noises of agreement, or the cooing of pigeons. He has the sense she is exerting a lot of energy to stay focused on what she is saying. Dr Järnfors has told him her mind often wanders, and her medication makes her tired, and sometimes confused.

She picks up her coffee cup with both hands and lifts it, slowly and shakily, to her lips. She drinks and exhales with pleasure. 'I spent a lot of time just wanting it to be over,' she says, 'but I kept losing my nerve. Then I went mad, and really didn't know what was happening from one day to the next.' She laughs, and for a moment the Eva Joe knew so long ago is sitting across from him.

'It's really you,' he says, saying the words without thinking. It is so strange to be sitting here with the woman who was once his wife.

'Yes, really me,' she says, 'an old granny. And you're really you, and old too.'

'I am,' Joe says, lifting his hands away from his body and looking down at his large belly.

'Am I, by the way?'

'Are you what?'

'A granny.'

'No,' he says. 'Marie's living with someone, but I don't think babies are on the horizon. She's at medical school. She's training to be a doctor.'

'Really?' She smiles for a moment then her face darkens. 'I hate doctors.'

'Aren't they the ones helping you get better?'

'They don't know what better is. All they do is fill me with drugs.'

'They say you're a lot better now than when you were admitted. What do you think?'

'Are you seeing anybody?' she says.

The question throws him. 'No,' he says. This isn't true, but he doesn't want to talk about that.

'Everybody needs someone,' she says, half-singing the words of a song Joe doesn't recognise. 'I have my doctors. Dr Järnfors, she's one,' Eva says, talking as if she knows something no one else has figured out. 'She says I should have been on medication years ago.'

'She didn't know you years ago,' Joe says, irritated. 'What are they giving you now?'

'Things with long and ugly names. An anti . . . anti-psykotisk?'

'Antipsychotic.'

'Yes, this. And a . . . antidepressant.'

'How do they make you feel?'

'Better sometimes, sometimes worse. I get headaches. I sweat.' She plucks at her baggy top.

They listen to the rain spatter on the glass. Eva makes small cooing sounds. A minute passes. Two minutes. Joe has run out of things to say, unless he tells her how miserable this all is. A line comes to him from somewhere: 'They hadn't grown apart; they had never really been together.' Is that true? He looks out at the leafless bushes that look like they are writhing in pain, the soil beneath them silvered with frost. It isn't true.

'Do you want to know what it's like?' Eva says, her voice suddenly seeming very loud in the empty cafeteria.

'Tell me.'

'When it comes it's like all the rules change. You feel everything falling apart and coming back together in new shapes, shapes you can't understand. You lose the ability to make sense of anything. You lose the will to get up out of the chair. You don't recognise your face in the mirror. Your breath stinks, your piss stinks. Everything seems thin, like it's made of paper. It's like a joke's been played on you, only it's terrifying, too. That's the worst part. You're terrified, on top of all the rest.'

'I can't imagine,' Joe says.

'You never could. You could only judge.'

It isn't Dr Järnfors's injunction that makes him temper his response, it's that he doesn't want to argue with this old, sick woman. 'I always tried my best not to feel anger towards you, Eva.'

As the conversation has gone on she has hunched more and more into herself, but at this she draws herself up. 'Did you? Did you really try?'

'I tried harder than you can guess.'

'Each time I left,' she says, 'it was the last thing I wanted to do. But it was the only thing that made sense. It was all I could do.' She darts her head down to her coffee cup. Joe finds her movements disconcerting, as he does the chain of coos she emits. Her head snaps up, startling him. 'You can't know what it's like for me,' she says. 'You can't, Marie can't. These doctors can't.' She smiles. 'It's OK. I know that.'

A few other people are coming into the cafeteria now, patients and medical staff. Lunchtime. The rain has stopped. Water drips from the bare bushes.

'There's a therapist here who takes us outside sometimes, into the birch forest. When it gets warmer I'll stay out there all day long. I've always loved those trees.'

Joe nods.

'She makes you write things, this woman,' Eva says.

'What kind of things?'

'Stories.'

'Made-up stories?'

'They can be made-up stories. Or stories about yourself, your feelings. They don't have to be "true" true. She says all stories, whatever they're about, are about you anyway. That every painting, whatever it shows, is a portrait of the artist.'

'You wrote a story?'

'Yes.'

'About what?'

'My mother. My childhood. A true story.'

Joe can tell she is proud of it. 'Marie always loved the way you told stories,' he says. 'Can I read it?'

The nurse who escorted Joe to the cafeteria, about whose presence he has completely forgotten, leans over and speaks to Eva in Swedish. She nods, raises her hand and says, 'Två minuter.'

The nurse looks at Joe and takes a few steps back from the table.

Eva returns her gaze to Joe. 'I want to see Marie,' she says. 'I demand it.'

'Demand?'

'Demand,' she says, continuing to stare and speaking slowly. 'I should never have been a mother, but Marie is my child and I cannot regret her. Have you even told her I'm here?'

'I told her. She said she didn't want to come.'

Eva's face slides downwards, as if her bones have crumbled. Joe hadn't planned to say it, but now it's out he can't take it back.

'Talk to her, Joe,' she says, tears spilling from her pale eyes. 'Talk to her for me.' She reaches her hands across the table to clasp his, but he doesn't take them. They remain there, trembling just above the table's surface.

'I can't force her, Eva, can I?' Joe says. Part of him is appalled at how reasonable he sounds.

Eva's mouth twitches. Her hands, held out before her, shake in the air. Then the nurse is beside them again, and Joe stands to leave. As Eva is led away he calls her name and the nurse turns her around. 'You are going to be a grandmother,' he says. 'In a few months.'

Eva smiles but uncertainly, as if she can no longer place who Joe is or why he is talking to her. She nods. 'Bra,' she says. Good.

#

Joe returns to London uncertain of what to do. If he tells Marie where Eva is she will go to her, immediately. Whatever anger she feels towards her, he knows it will all drain away when they are face to face. The thought enrages him. Why does she deserve forgiveness after causing so much pain? He promised that he would never let Eva hurt Marie again. This is his chance to honour that promise. Or is it revenge?

A week later his options are taken away. When he hears a voice tell him Eva is dead, his first thought is that she has finally taken the step she so often talked about. But no, it was a heart attack caused by a bleeding ulcer.

Joe tells Marie Eva was admitted to a hospital before she died, but he doesn't say how long before. The staff did some detective work, he says. He is almost disappointed that she doesn't challenge his version of events, that she doesn't say 'You saw her, didn't you? She wanted to see me, didn't she?' She accepts what he tells her as the truth. A time will come when he'll tell her, he thinks, after the baby is born, but for now he busies himself with organisation: flights, a cremation, and a sapling in a remembrance garden, a birch. The day before they fly a package arrives from Sweden. Expecting something administrative he is surprised to find a small pile of papers inside, with a Post-it attached:

You said you wanted to read it, so here it is.
Eva

Beneath the Post-it is the title: 'Sommar 1976'. He lifts the title sheet and looks at the first page, then the next: it's written in Swedish. He laughs, drops the papers onto the table and sits down. He thinks of Eva in the days after his visit, hoping Marie would change her mind. He thinks of her in her room at night, listening to the zoo animals call to one another. He puts his face in his hands. Much later, a translation app open beside him, he begins to read.

ACKNOWLEDGEMENTS

I want to thank Heath Branigan, Jake Leighton-Pope and Toby Leighton-Pope for making me put my keyboard where my mouth was. Natasha Soobramanien for doing so much to help these stories walk at an early, crucial stage. Colin Barrett, Brendan Barrington, David Hayden, Yiyun Li, Alison Macleod, Jon McGregor, Nuala Ní Chonchúir and Luke Williams for your careful reading and invaluable guidance. Eva Järnfors, for telling me about the apple. Emma Mitchell for letting me sniff your spirit gum. Jessica Burdon for talking to me at that party. Jesica Uzureau, Fernanda Adame, Valeria Farill and Marisol Cal y Mayor for christening Nuria. Leo Robson for counsel and noodles. Maria Garbutt-Lucero and everyone at Faber for making me feel so welcome. Emmie Francis, all I could want in an editor. My agent Emma Paterson, and my agent past, Jack Ramm, for being true allies. And Sofia, Astrid and Sigrid: the greatest.